BEAR V SHARK

BEAR V SHARK

CHRIS BACHELDER

BLOOMSBURY

First published in Great Britain 2002

Copyright © 2001 by Chris Bachelder

The moral right of the author has been asserted

Bloomsbury Publishing Plc, 38 Soho Square, London W1D 3HB

A CIP catalogue record for this book is available from the British Library

ISBN 0 7475 5992 9

10 9 8 7 6 5 4 3 2 1

Printed in Great Britain by Clays Ltd, St Ives plc

For my mother, Linda Wilson
For my father, Allen Bachelder
and
For my sister, Lisa Bachelder

Acknowledgments

Hearty thanks to Gillian Blake and Rachel Sussman at Scribner for their expertise and enthusiasm, and to Lisa Bankoff for getting the book in the right hands.

Thanks to extraordinary teachers: Michael Parker, Greg Meyerson, and especially Padgett Powell, who talked big and backed it up.

Many thanks to my talented and generous peers in the UF writing workshop, and in particular to Emily Miller, a remarkable friend.

Deluxe thanks to Rob Seals, an inspiration. A bear hug to Cynthia Nearman, big-hearted comrade.

Thanks to Florrie for her warm hospitality, to Joyce for her kindness and her faith in good things, to Ron for the big idea.

Special thanks to Kate Moulder for all that she gave.

And most of all, thanks to my parents and sister for their love, trust, and support. I shut up and took it all.

Lord Clifford says, "The smallest worm will turn being trodden upon."

—King Henry VI, Part III

Kurt Vonnegut Jr. says, "This is meant to be optimistic, I think, but I have to tell you that a worm can be stepped on in such a way that it can't possibly turn after you remove your foot."

—Address to graduating class at
Bennington College

Bear v. Shark: The Preface

Bear v. Shark: The Novel is based on a *true story*.

Or, rather: It is *based on* a true story.

Imagine a true story. Imagine this true story in a solid, middle-class neighborhood, modest and truthful. Imagine its joists, its beams, the steady, cautious slope of its shingled roof. Imagine its crisp, righteous corners, those near-perfect 90-degree angles, knowing as you do that a perfect 90-degree angle—like a perfect circle or a perfect butt—doesn't really exist in the Real World, but knowing that these angles have aspired to perfection, nonetheless (or else what's a heaven for?). Imagine the clean closets, the sensible floor plan, the utter lack of luxury or flourish. Imagine that the materials are first-rate, chosen and guaranteed by men who care about doing a job right dammit. Imagine that everything checks out, yes the basement is unfinished and dank, but it's the truth, take it or leave it.

Good.

Now, imagine, based atop this monument to forthrightness and plain dealing, imagine a ramshackle unit constructed willy-nilly, catch-as-catch-can, higgledy-piggledy, all pastiched together with hyphens and the thin, colorful threads of ideas, a motley edifice, part bungalow, part high-rise, part rambler, there's stucco and brick and wood and vinyl siding, not unplanned, *not* unplanned, *charming* or *interesting* being the absolute best way to describe this place if you're standing on the bushwhacked front lawn of Truth, not unstable in its own right but perched upon, based on, the cautious, steady slope of the shingled roof of Truth and teetering, teetering, the whole damn situation fixing to collapse into tainted wreckage, in which wreckage lie nearly equal parts Truth and Lie, Irony and That Which Is Not Irony, such that context and purity are forever lost, and the pieces are indistinguishable.

How shall I regard that naily 2 by 4? Is it a metaplank, a super-plank, a plank self-referential? A complex and ambiguous plank, and all the more so for its apparent simplicity, its garish honesty regarding its own dimensions? Has anyone even bothered to measure the 2 by 4? In short: Is this a postmodern stick?

Say, are we to look *through* or *at* that cracked window?

Linoleum: Authenticity or the death of authenticity?

Imagine that.

and now this . . .

Part One

The Broad, Flapping
American Ear

1

Parlor Game

So it's kind of like a parlor game, then? In essence?
I guess so.
Well that sounds fun. Bear against Shark.
It's Bear *v.* Shark. What's a parlor?
Oh . . . You know, a parlor. A *parlour*.
. . . ?
Um, like a salon.
What?
A lounge, essentially.
A *lounge* game?
Well, you know, it's like where you play it.
What's a parlor?
Like a living room. Technically.
Parlor?
Yes.
In a building?
In a home.
How big a TV you put in there?

2

Whiteout

The Television, the couch, the main character (Mr. Norman) asleep, twitching in the strobe glow.

The Television says don't you go away, we'll be right back.

Mr. Norman is all twitch and mutter. He doesn't go away.

There's American-style shag carpet and there's wood paneling wallpaper, I couldn't tell the difference, you fooled me, where's the seam?

It's morning, rise and shine.

And then from dreams grainy and edge-blurry, cold-sizzling with synaptic crack and static, Mr. Norman opens his eyes into the titillating snow-white throb of a cordless vibrating pillow, the Vibra-Dream Plus, not available in stores, order today.

This blindingly white pillow, for which operators are standing by, cradles Mr. Norman's face and curves seductively, ergonomically, up to his ears, into which it purrs and coos like a lover.

The pillow-lover says, "Three easy payments."

She says, "For a limited time only, void where prohibited, ergonomically designed."

She says, "Check the cordless pillow aisle at your local grocer."

On Television it's the same thing.

Ergonomically: from the Latin *ergo* (therefore) and the French *nom* (name).

Into the soft white fleece of his virgin lover Mr. Norman says, "Therefore name?"

She (the pillow) doesn't care whether Mr. Norman used Visa or MasterCard, or whether he ordered by toll-free number or via the Internet or even through the painfully and deliciously slow U.S. Postal Service. She (the pillow) just wants Mr. Norman to rest easy after a long day at the office. She understands. She cares. She grazes his earlobes when she speaks.

With her thrumming tongue, her tingling lips, the pillow-lover says, "Therefore name." It makes sense.

Her design? Well, her design combines Old World Comfort with Space Age Materials. She is the official cordless pillow of Bear v. Shark II.

Mr. Norman's neck hurts, but she (the revolutionary pillow of tomorrow) says, "You be still, big boy."

She says, "Stain resistant, lab tested, stylish durability."

Mr. Norman, penis erect and warranty expired, remains facedown on the couch in the big Television room of his suburban home, his eyes squinting into a whiteout of sexy sleep technology, a hot blizzard of affordable comfort and Yankee can-do know-how.

In a manner of speaking: Mr. Norman wakes up.

3

Ohms and Amperes

A wife (Mrs. Norman) and two boys all asleep upstairs.

We got ourselves a quiet house. This suburban house is completely and blessedly silent.

One thinks of wind-kissed meadows. One thinks of bomb shelters.

The house is completely silent, except only for those trifling noises against which we recognize and understand the very idea of silence, the rustle and pulse that we might say define silence, yes, bring it into existence and lock it into a paired opposition that confers meaning and context.

The silent house: silent, that is, except for the chemical hum of the central air-conditioning, except for the hiss of dehumidifiers, except for the Babelic chatter of Televisions.

Silent but for the synthetic pulse of coaxial cables, converters, underground fiber-optic lines. The crackle and pop of electricity, currency, frequency—the ohms and amperes, watts and volts.

All silent except for the thud of the *Land Swaps & Divorces* against vinyl siding, except for the clicking of the hard drive, the murmuring of Web site authors—Charles Lindbergh deniers, child pornographers, auctioneers, insomniacs, quilters, Captains of Industry, professors of Canadian Literature.

Except for the gunshots, the sirens, the gunshots, the choppers.

Except for bear banter, shark schlock.

Except for the inexorable grind of continental plates miles below the earth's surface.

Miles?

Silent except for the utopian drone of the Vibra-Dream Plus and the sweet, sweet morning songs of electric birds installed in the imitation dogwoods in the backyard of Mr. Norman's suburban cable-ready home.

Fax, scanner, cell phone.

You shoot a bear so many times and it still doesn't die.

The house is completely silent when Mr. Norman awakes.

4

Lady v. Cake

On the Television, on a Television, a lady lawyer in a low-cut silk blouse is cross-examining a chocolate cake.

The lady lawyer, pacing like TV lawyers will, has great calves, a nice thin waist, full-bodied hair, no panty lines. All of the lady lawyer's unwanted hair is offscreen somewhere, removed and hidden in bloody wastepaper baskets, unwanted. She looks fantastic, but a little crazy in the eyes, a little sharp in the nose and chin, a little too aggressive, a little too skeptical of modern dessert technology.

The chocolate cake—seated up at the witness stand in front of a microphone and next to a stern, fair-minded, balding, middle-aged white male TV commercial judge (the other two types of TV commercial judges being [1] a stern, fair-minded, middle-aged, gray-haired white woman and [2] a stern, fair-minded black woman, any age)—the cake, I say, looks every bit as hot as the lady lawyer, and innocent to boot. This chocolate cake appears utterly incapable of the smallest misdemeanor.

The cake is rich, luscious, moist, exotically frosted. From the courtroom scene cut to a close-up of the nude cake being sliced open, its moistness revealed in pornographic slow motion. This cake is begging to be frosted. She (this cake) is both vixen and virgin. She is perfect: women want to identify with her, create her and thus re-create themselves, mix her and bake her at 375°, fill the kitchen with her sweet perfume.

Men want to devour her.

Cut back to the courtroom scene.

The lady lawyer says, "If it is indeed true that you are from a mix, would you mind telling the jury just how you got to be so creamy?"

There's a little boy in the Normans' front yard. The front yards around here are paved and painted green. The grass doesn't do so well.

Facedown in the Vibra-Dream Plus, Mr. Norman does not know: Was Grizzly Adams the name of the bearded guy or the bear?

5

The Old Televisions, Part I

The old Televisions had an off switch.

6

Ten Myths about Babbling

Man on a couch, beached and chatty.

He (Mr. Norman) says, "That's probably not going to be enough for a first down."

He says, "Plantigrade gait, liquidation sale, murder-suicide."

An expert says, "We believe that it is generally most severe in the mornings."

Four out of five experts say, "We recommend Babble Blocker, a prescription drug."

Nobody says, "Isn't the pharmaceutical company part of the same conglomerate as the Television networks?"

The Babble Blocker pamphlet, "Ten Myths about Babbling," says:

Myth No. 3: People who babble are "nutbags." (Fact: Logorrhea has nothing to do with sanity or intelligence. The institutionalization of babblers is generally no longer accepted as the best method of treatment. Most babblers can lead productive lives, and some even achieve greatness.)

Mr. Norman says, "Liquor? I hardly know her."

Myth No. 5: I must be the only person in the world who babbles. (Fact: You are not alone. Over 10 million Americans have been diagnosed with logorrhea.)

The evil sexy lady lawyer badgers the cake. She's a real bitch. She says, "You sit there all sweet and scrumptious, and you expect us to believe that you are *fat free*?"

Mr. Norman says not all antifungal ointments are the same.

Myth No. 8: Babble Blocker turns you into a "zombie" and also slowly erodes your kidneys. (Fact: Although BB tends to induce lethargy, glassy-eyed compliance, and kidney erosion in laboratory rats and monkeys, recent longitudinal studies suggest that humans do not suffer these same side effects to nearly the same extent. Side effects include: dry mouth, headaches, ennui, vomiting, ejaculatory failure, sweating, irritability, color blindness, and memory loss.)

Someone, maybe in the kitchen or the small Television room, says now take a look at the stain on the right.

Myth No. 10: There's no cure for babbling.

The cross-examined cake, of course, is polite, demure, sheepish, nonconfrontational, sexy as all *get-out*. She (the chocolate cake) says, "Yes, ma'am."

Yes, ma'am: The phrase has caught on with the kids. Hipsters in Chicago, Wheeling (West Virginia), and Beijing go around imitating that cake: *Yes, ma'am. Yes, ma'am.* It means the same thing as, say, "cool" or "right on" or "you're shittin' me." There is a Web site devoted to Lady v. Cake, fifteen thousand hits per day. There are Internet chat rooms, where people from all nations meet to discuss the finer points of law and food porn.

The cake is on a book-signing tour.

7

Mile Marker No. 68

All this silence is getting to Mr. Norman.

His neck hurts, he feels restless. He lifts his face out of the warm lap of the Vibra-Dream Plus, despite her protestations, her seductive offers and money-back guarantees.

On TV a man in a tuxedo is sprinting through a sunny neighborhood with an ice cream cone.

Mr. Norman works in an office, but not today. He works on a team that designs fake electronic equipment for model apartments and town homes, but not today. Today is a vacation day.

Mr. Norman feels like running a ten-kilometer race. That is how far? Ten kilometers is roughly 10,000 meters, a meter is roughly a yard, a yard is roughly three feet, a mile is . . . What the hell is a country mile? What about a nautical mile? How would a crow fly under water?

League, stadium, fathom.

No, a marathon, or an *ultramarathon,* one of those 100-mile races through the desert. Mr. Norman saw that once on the Outrageous Accomplishments Network, these people running 100 miles, running from something or toward something, who knows, just running for days and drinking literally pints and pints of fluids. These gaunt fellows: what have they figured out?

The design team doesn't do fake plants. That's another office.

They just do fake electronic equipment. For model apartments and town homes. Well, it started out for model apartments and town homes, but lately regular folks have been buying the fake equipment because it looks better than the real equipment and it is competitively priced.

Mr. Norman imagines himself in the white-hot sands, covered with the crusty white residue of his sweat, the vultures circling in the high white heat above. His eyes are fixed, his face is placid, serene. He has found something, he has reached some sort of enlightenment, out there in the desert at Mile Marker No. 68. He has passed through pain and he has found something sublime, the IT, the NOW, it's like buying a Lexus or getting drunk, only better, more Eastern. It's Extreme Zen. In this moment of transcendence, Mr. Norman's shorts and singlet and shoes would be sporty, yet durable and functional. They would *breathe*. The logo would be recognized internationally.

The design team knows nothing about electronic equipment except the way it looks. Team members scour gadget catalogs like porno mags. They have to keep up with technology. They have to keep up with the way technology looks. Team members e-mail each other when they have new ideas about how to make a fake piece of equipment look more real than a real piece of equipment.

Oh, and then the choice that every Ultra Athlete faces at one time or another: Should I break my rhythm and my concentration for a short bathroom break or just piss on myself? Mr. Norman wonders if pissing on himself would impress his sponsors or just turn them off. You could really see it both ways. He supposes it could be edited out if they didn't like it. Fake Televisions, fake VCRs, fake CD players, fake laptops. Mr. Norman wants to suck down a tube of Dr. Endurance Energy Goo and throw it in the sand.

Mr. Norman can't remember the last time he ran, even a few steps.

He says, "Ninety days, same as cash."

He says, "How many meters in an odometer?"

A TV Personality in the spare Television room says, "Did you know, Gloria, that the origin of the teddy bear comes more or less from Franklin Delanor Roosevelt?"

With great effort, Mr. Norman turns himself over on the couch. He lies on his back now, the pillow-lover picking up where she left off, the electric birds going at it in the imitation dogwoods. He folds his arms over his chest. He sees the cacti (asparagi, octopi, walri), he feels the brutal sun a million miles away. Ten million, whatever, it's a star like other stars, gaseous, bigger than Jupiter, involved in photosynthesis. He thinks the hot urine might feel good streaming down his sinewy enlightened legs. Or maybe it would feel bad. Either way.

As he does every morning, he vomits sentences, phrases, jingles, until there are just words, then syllables, a long, dry, incomprehensible heave.

That little kid in the front yard walks tight figure eights with his head down. He stops occasionally, stares up at the Normans' dark house.

She (Gloria) says, "Trent, my kids love their teddy sharks. They just love them."

Mr. Norman becomes aware of his heartbeat. With his hands on his chest he can feel his own four-chambered heart pumping blood and riboflavin throughout his body.

Turns out it isn't shaped like a heart.

Capillaries, aorta, ventricle, plate tectonics, Valentine's Day.

Somewhere a gun says, "Flesh is weak, motherfucker."

Somewhere a siren says, "You just wouldn't believe what they can do with artificial limbs these days."

Somewhere a diamond pendant says, "I love you."

A bald guy on the Pundit Network says it's not a matter of whether we distribute guns in the schools, but when.

Seven chapters and the guy hasn't gotten off the couch yet.

In the palms of his folded hands, Mr. Norman feels the beating, the beating, the creepy beating of heart under bone.

8

Four-Minute Guarantee

Here at News 8 we know you live a busy, hectic life. We know that you juggle work and entertainment and family, and that your time is your most precious natural resource.

Most other stations give you the day's news in six minutes, but in our crazy and hectic world, who has time for six minutes of news? That's why we at News 8 give you our Four-Minute Guarantee. You give us four minutes and we'll give you the planet. Weather, sports, news, and in-depth analysis of current events—all in four minutes or our name isn't News 8.

And tonight after News 8 join us for our ongoing series, *Bear v. Shark: The Tale of the Tape.* Tonight we focus on the tongue factor. Do sharks have one? Tune in at 10:04.

9

Patented Comfort System

Not even light yet, Mr. Norman roaming his house, socks on carpet, the soft rustle like artificial sweetener in decaf. Room to room to room, I mean, a bear, yes, of course, would and can, but a shark does and just might, also.

Rows of triangular teeth.

On TV, well, a man and a woman. *Together.* Vigorously and imaginatively. Is that her *leg*? And what's *that*? Is she having the time of her life or is he hurting her? Are they in love, these people on the greasy counter of the fast food restaurant? Not the characters, who after all just met ("Can I take your order?" "OK, bend over"), but the *actors,* are the actors in love? Do they live together in a ranch-style house on the edge of town, a give-and-take marital situation, all about compromise and communication—communication is *key*— with knickknacks on shelves, photos in albums, this eerie deal where each finishes the other's sentences? Is their lovemaking gentle, traditional? Face-to-face and with no animals or power tools?

In the hallway Mr. Norman pauses, sees the televised sex act reflected on the sad gray face of the family's old broken TV. I'm afraid it's gone, a guy in a jumpsuit had said six months ago. The use of condiments in that way, it requires love, does it not? Love and trust? Or hatred and vengeance? Or massive indifference? It requires something. Man, look out, here comes the manager and he's not wearing pants.

Mr. Norman. Up the stairs to his sons' room. A poster on the door, a collage of tooth and claw, *Do Not Enter*. Mr. Norman enters.

Curtis in his fake bearskin sleeping bag giggles and says, "Ruptured Achilles tendon."

Matthew looks sullen even in sleep. Like he thinks sleeping is stupid.

Both children are breathing in and out. They're alive. Something in the room is beeping not rhythmically. Electronic football beeps like that. Basketball, too. Electronic war also beeps like that, and so does laser archery. Sleeping kids: the blank, naked faces, unstimulated. Mr. Norman feels he should feel something. He *does* feel a little something, yes, there it is, and he wonders if it is a flood of love. There it is again. That would seem to be the logical thing, looking at one's sleeping children, a flood of love, but what does a love flood feel like? Would he know one? Is it often mistaken for indigestion? Are there tests? Is there a *battery* of tests? Can we rule anything out? Does a love flood leave behind soggy scraps of sentiment, glistening on the banks of your heart?

Beep beep. Beep.

Mr. Norman goes to his bedroom, his handsome wife. Through the blinds are those the first rays of a glorious new day? Is that the Life Giver rising yonder in the East? No. It's just a streetlight. The metallic frames of bedside photographs gleam, but the pictures remain black, inscrutable. Mr. Norman can't remember the images inside those frames. Probably him, Mrs. Norman, the boys, squinting in sunshine, mouths turned up to resemble smiles.

Mr. Norman sits on the edge of the mattress, which is really a patented comfort system with microcoils that overlap and interlock like chapters in a novel.

Mrs. Norman turns in her sleep. She says, "What?"

Mr. Norman says, "I mean, just think about it."

Mrs. Norman says, "You're here."

Mr. Norman says, "Be as honest as you can."

Mrs. Norman says, "Right now. Let's."

Mr. Norman says, "Promise?"

Mrs. Norman used to be such a great water skier. It's not like she could do fancy tricks, it's just that she was so graceful and easy on the water. Smiling in the spray.

She says nothing but sort of moans from the back of her throat.

Her head rests on the merest suggestion of a pillow, just the *idea* of a pillow, really, the UnPillow, lost in a standard-size case, wafer thin and neck friendly, eighty-five dollars plus s&h. Mrs. Norman is a disciple of Posture.

Mr. Norman looks up at the dark ceiling. He says, "I just need to know."

Mrs. Norman says, "I'm right over here."

Mr. Norman crawls under the comforter, but he's on top of the lightweight, wrinkle-free sheet and his wife is underneath it and he can't find her and they toss and wrestle and grunt, while the mattress subtly conforms and adjusts to their marriage. That's not her breast, it's her shoulder, and soon she's mumbling and sleep-breathing again, her patented spinal corset creaking slightly with each breath.

Mr. Norman in the dark. It's going to be a big day, a big weekend. If something is wrong, and I'm not saying something is wrong, but if something is wrong, it will be set right this weekend. Won't it?

Mr. Norman says, "Honey."

The bedside photographs like small broken Televisions.

Mr. Norman says, "Honey, am I *fun*?"

10

Bear v. Shark: The Question

The question is simple, as are most profound questions.

Given a relatively level playing field—i.e., water deep enough so that a Shark could maneuver proficiently, but shallow enough so that a Bear could stand and operate with its characteristic dexterity—who would win in a fight between a Bear and a Shark?

11

Weather Europe

You should know by now: The Normans of America are going to Las Vegas for The Sequel: Darwin's Duel, Surf against Turf, Lungs v. Gills in the Neon Desert for All the Marbles.

Mrs. Norman and the two boys, Matthew and Curtis, are awake. They're getting ready, it's pretty exciting.

Mrs. Norman's electronic mail message says, "This is going to be fun!" It (the electronic message) says, "Don't forget to pack underwear and a toothbrush."

Mrs. Norman comes downstairs. Her posture is remarkable, it's something she's worked on. She says to Mr. Norman, "How was your day?"

Mr. Norman says, "What?"

Mrs. Norman says, "Oh."

She says, "How did you sleep?"

Mr. Norman says, "There was an interesting program last night on the Great Wall of China. Turns out it's technically a hologram. It's the largest man-made hologram."

Mrs. Norman says, "What do you mean by technically?"

Mr. Norman says, "You mind if I turn up the birds?"

Mrs. Norman says, "I dreamed that I found a turtle and I knew I had a CD stuck in him but I couldn't figure out how to get it out. It was so frustrating because I knew the CD was inside there, it was that Mall Sonatas one I like so much. Inside the turtle."

Matthew, the older boy, comes downstairs. Colorful sharks circle his pajamas and lunge at fat lazy seals. He has cut off the sleeves, apparently with dull scissors or a knife.

Mr. Norman checks the Internet for the weather. He wants to check the weather on the Television, too. He asks Matthew to turn the Television to the weather network.

Matthew sighs and says, "Which one?"

Mr. Norman says, "The one on the staircase."

Matthew says, "Not which Television, which weather network?"

Mr. Norman says, "How many are there?"

Matthew scowls. It's a difficult age. Or maybe something is wrong with him. Or maybe this is just normal. He says, "There's the Weather Network and there's Weather Network Plus and there's Extreme Weather."

Mrs. Norman is sitting right-angled in the kitchen Net Nook, printing a course map and checking the weather on the Internet. She says, "There's also Weather Europe."

Mr. Norman says, "What's the difference?"

Matthew says, "Weather Europe is not a part of our cable package."

Curtis appears downstairs with a briefcase.

Mrs. Norman says, "Cable package."

Mr. Norman says, "Just put it on the Weather Network."

Matthew says, "I've said it so many times and I'll say it again. The Weather Network Plus is better."

Mr. Norman says, "Why is it better?"

Matthew says, "What it is is more up-to-the-minute and complete."

Mr. Norman says, "More complete than twenty-four hours a day?"

Matthew says, "It has more weather."

Mrs. Norman says, "I wonder why they even have the Weather Network anymore."

Curtis says, "Extreme Weather has this thing where they show you the weather from the weather's perspective. It looks awesome."

Mr. Norman says, "Put it on Weather Network Plus."

Matthew says, "I have no idea what channel that is."

Mrs. Norman (in the Net Nook) says, "Just a sec, I'll check our local cable listings for details."

12

The Old Televisions, Part II

The point being: Watching Television used to be a distinct and bounded activity, like bowling or extreme virtual snowboarding. You were not doing it and then you were doing it. Likewise, you were doing it and then you were not doing it. On, off. Off, on. 0, 1. Binary: simple, discrete, delineated. You turned it on to watch and you turned it off when you were finished. When you were finished, you turned it off. Seems so strange now. That one-inch heavy plastic border around the screen, everyone thought it was a nonpermeable membrane. It would have been silly to suggest otherwise. But here's the thing: as the images on the screen kept getting brighter, sharper, clearer, the Television Set's plastic border kept getting fuzzier, blurrier, more ill-defined. The spilled images shimmered and danced in American parlors. Television became, gradually, nondiscrete. Watching Television became, gradually, nonbinary. TV got tangled up in our lives, and there was no untangling. Our lives, which are on continuously (until they are off). You don't turn a life on and off, off and on, on and off. Likewise with a TV, which is bound to life inseparably, inextricably. You wouldn't (and couldn't) turn it off even if you could. And you can't—because there is no off switch, because the Televisions are built into the walls of homes, because they are in stores and restaurants, mounted in the corners above your booth, spilling pixels into your porridge. And most of all, because they are there (and on) even when they are not there. Did you ever see that one episode of *American Nightmare* where the insane guy wants to turn off his Television? And there's no off switch and there's no cord to pull out? And he's going crazy, running around, screaming? It's spooky, kind of, but it's also hilarious. He's running around with this wild look and finally he gets a gun and he stands in front of the big screen and he fires a shot right into it. And we're at floor level looking up at the screen—the crazy guy's screen—and we see it like explode and we hear something fall to the ground and then we see the crazy guy's foot twitching at the bottom right of our screen. Through our screen we see his exploded screen and his foot. And when the cops come later, they find the guy on the floor with a single bullet through his head. That's a cool one.

13

Dew Point

Mr. Norman staring at the Television on the staircase. Red arrows and blue arrows battle for meteorological supremacy. Clouds and decimal points race along coastlines. Happy yellow suns, happier and yellower than real suns, are scattered across a map. The suns have smiley faces, even though they are leaving burn marks in the earth.

There is a thunderstorm warning, a heat advisory, a wind alert, a smog watch, a pollen alarm, a low-pressure trough, an Appalachian wedge, a hurricane stage three. There is weather *everywhere*. Weather is assaulting this defenseless planet and it's like nobody gives a damn.

In the top right corner of the Television is a small box tuned to a different channel. Picture in picture: Extreme Weather's award-winning weathermentary, *Tsunami Tsurvival!* Slow-motion footage of a piece of rice slicing through a car door.

Mrs. Norman walks by. She says, "Interesting footage."

Damn right, it's unbelievable footage, we're talking never-before-seen footage. Mr. Norman is pretty interested in the footage, but there's Matthew staring, impassive, unimpressed. Something's not right.

Sometimes Mr. Norman has the vague feeling that Matthew is gay. He thinks he would be OK with his son's homosexuality, just fine. When the time comes he would have a talk with him.

Mr. Norman might say, "Son, I'm straight but not narrow."

He would say, "Matty, hate is NOT a family value."

He might add, "I'm glad we had this talk. Celebrate diversity."

Mr. Norman says, "I think it's raining."

Curtis, the younger boy, whose scholastic efforts have earned the Normans this trip to Las Vegas, a pudgy child, unathletic, unequivocally pro-Bear, a good kid, friendly, outgoing, not much of a reader, a pretty decent PlayMax Extreme Death Match player, says, "What?"

Mr. Norman says, "I think it's raining." To himself he adds, "Gay pride."

Sedge Kellerman, the weather guy, says, "The Bear Index (BI) refers to how hot a bear would be at this temperature."

Picture in picture: Asian youngsters whistling through a schoolyard like bullets. Pretty stock footage.

Curtis says, "No, I was just outside putting the satellite dish on the Sport Utility Vehicle. It's threatening, but it's not raining."

Mr. Norman says, "But look at this satellite photo."

Mrs. Norman, up from the Net Nook, stares at the Television on the staircase. She says, "That's a satellite photo of Finland."

Curtis (the younger boy) says, "Are they the Dutch?"

Mr. Norman says, "What is barometric pressure?"

Curtis says, "My teacher says the Dutch don't have a culture anymore. It's been taken away."

Matthew says, "What I'm asking you is who would want the Dutch culture?"

Curtis says, "Her gardener is a Dutch and he's bitter and kind of hunched over and he says the culture has been sucked bloodless."

Mrs. Norman is so upright she's almost leaning backward.

Sedge says, "It looks like clear weather today for our pilots. It's a good day for air strikes, Chuck."

Mrs. Norman says, "Barometric pressure is how hard the sky is pressing down on us."

Mr. Norman says, "But gravity is a constant. That's one of Newton's quips."

The younger boy, Curtis, says, "It turns out that Newton may not really have gotten an apple shot off of his head."

Mrs. Norman says, "Then what's dew point?"

Mr. Norman's older son (Matthew) says, "Wooden shoes and tulips and fjords? No thanks, you can have it."

Chuck (Sedge's co-anchor on the TWN Plus morning shift) says, "Good luck, boys. Come home with your shield or on it."

Mr. Norman says, "Turns out the record high for today is only eighty-five."

Matthew says, "Is that metric or what?"

Curtis says, "I think that's Weather Europe, Dad."

Sedge Kellerman says, "Now back to Gail at the Humidity Desk."

Mrs. Norman checks the Internet. She says it turns out that the Dutch have worked hard to retain a thriving, vibrant culture.

14

Question-and-Answer Period

Upstairs, a bright-toothed, square-jawed young man in a hooded raincoat shares a split screen with a button-cute Television Personality. They're both going places, you can just see it.

She (Lee Ann Cordero) says, Let's check in with Trevor Foxx out at the Singer Outdoor Pavilion. Well, Trevor, looks like you need gills out there.

All I want to know is, are these two doing it or not?

He (Trevor Foxx) says, Ha, ha. That's right, Lee Ann.

Lee Ann says, Trevor, tell us what you've seen out there this morning. I mean, besides slanty rain.

Trevor Foxx says, Well, Lee Ann, an estimated crowd of 10,000 braved the wretched weather today to attend Reverend Marty Munson's special address here at the Singer Outdoor Pavilion. Reverend Munson, who was paroled last week, spoke for about an hour, primarily about the importance of faith in today's hectic world. He also urged the people to send their prayers to the families of the mudslide victims in Mexico City and to the refugees in Illinois.

Damn, you know they're doing it. And they deserve one another, such beautiful people.

Lee Ann Cordero says, Trevor, did the Reverend appear to be in good health?

Trevor Foxx smiles.

Lee Ann Cordero says, Trevor?

Trevor Foxx smiles. Those *teeth*.

Lee Ann Cordero says, Trevor?

Trevor Foxx turns to his right. He says, Are we still on?

Lee Ann Cordero says, We appear to be having what we in the business call technical difficulties.

Trevor says, I guess not.

Lee Ann says, We'll get this straightened out and get back to Trevor as soon as possible.

Trevor says, Gills, that's real funny. Barbie sits on her big ass in that studio, while I'm in this goddamn monsoon. If I had cleavage like that, you think I'd keep getting passed over?

Maybe they were doing it at one time and are no longer doing it.

Trevor shrugs and then peers into the monitor, tilting his head sideways. He says, I wish I could grow sideburns. One side comes in fine, but the other side is like the fucking mange or something.

Lee Ann says, Thank you, Trevor, for that report.

Trevor Foxx looks back at the camera. He says, Lee Ann?

Lee Ann says, Trevor?

Trevor Foxx says, Lee Ann?

It's pretty obvious they still have feelings for one another. You can't help but pull for them.

Trevor Foxx says, Lee Ann, in a question-and-answer period after Reverend Munson's talk, someone asked him if God is rooting for the bear or the shark. Reverend Munson drew a mixed and vocal response when he said that he had had plenty of time in the slammer to think about this question and he had decided that God loves all of his creatures equally—but just maybe He loves bears a little more.

Lee Ann says, Interesting, Trevor.

Trevor says, Back to you, Lee Ann.

Lee Ann says, Thanks, Trevor, and go get yourself some hot soup.

15

Bear v. Shark:
The Breakfast Cereal

Family vacation, big day, it's important to start your day off, you know, *right*.

If you can't have a nutritious breakfast, then at least have something that is an important part of one.

The Normans all together except for maybe one of the kids, sitting at the kitchen table in front of a Television like families used to, damn Rockwell print here.

The kid outside is at the edge of the lawn, pretending to juggle four sharp objects.

Chocolate waffle bears, chewy caramel sharks, and little marshmallows in the shapes of lawyers, guns, and money. Shark Pup Scratch-N-Sniff in Specially Marked Boxes.

The cereal box (Specially Marked) says, "Now available in Family Size and Today's Hectic World Size."

The cereal box says, "Kids love the taste, adults love the mid-morning competitive advantage that it confers."

The cereal box says, "Did you hear the one about the foolhardy mouse who clicked on a sleeping bear? (Punch line inside!)"

The cereal box says, "Provides 75% of your daily nougat and 100% of your daily fun!"

The cereal box says, "Warning: Pregnant women should not eat the marshmallows."

The cereal box says, "Test your knowledge of bears and sharks with this fun True or False quiz."

The cereal box says, "Wallace might have beaten Darwin to it if he'd only had an entertaining and nutritious breakfast!"

The cereal box says, "Visit our Web site."

The cereal box says, "Free pager inside."

The cereal box says, "Ten simple things you can do to cut down on mass starvation."

Mrs. Norman says, "Well, I guess we should get the car loaded."

The punch line (inside!) says, "The bear didn't get mad, he got even. He waited until the mouse and his family were all asleep inside their den and then he burst in and opened fire, killing everyone. Sweet revenge!"

The Television says Bear v. Shark Cereal is the official cereal of Bear v. Shark II.

One of the boys says the way he heard it was that the bear hacked the mouse family up with one of those curvy-bladed Grim Reaper–type deals.

Machete?

No, a scythe.

16

Lucky Marble

The Normans load the Sport Utility Vehicle (SUV). There is no rain. The morning sky is sky blue. Bloated, billowy clouds float gently across the sky like dead fish in a lake. The sky is not so much blue as it is brown.

Someone says, Cumulative clouds.

Someone says, Calamari olives, tubal litigation, ulterior motif.

Curtis says, "That one looks like a derringer."

Matthew turns his head sideways and stares at the bloated fish-clouds. He says, "It looks more like a battle-ax to me."

Curtis says, "No, not that one. Over here. See the harpoon? It's just to the left of that."

Matthew says, "Whatever."

Mrs. Norman checks the thermometer on the side of the house. She says, "Golly, no wonder it's so hot."

The e-atlas says it's 812 miles to Las Vegas. It recommends that the Normans take two days to get there (Thursday and Friday), which gives them much of Saturday to see the sights in what is often referred to as the World's Most Amusing Country. The big show is Saturday night at the Darwin Dome—9 P.M. Eastern Standard Time, 6 P.M. Pacific.

The e-atlas recommends that the Normans visit the World's Largest Billboard, the World's Funnest Virtual Water Park, and the

World's Original Gambling Monkey, all of which are located within the Museum of Las Vegas Secession.

The families in the houses on each side of the Normans' house gather at curtained, pressure-treated windows to peek out high and low at the lucky American family next door. Think about it, it could have been us. What's so special about the Normans? It *should* have been us. Dammit, why can't our family go to Las Vegas to be healed and entertained? The disappointments in this life just stack up.

Mr. Norman looks at his front yard. He thinks it is beginning to crack, chip, and peel. He thinks it is beginning to flake and fade. It is not a healthy lawn.

He hoists suitcases into the SUV. He says, "How did you get the CD out?"

Mrs. Norman says, "What?"

Mr. Norman, his dental work tingling and popping with colorless, odorless waves of data, says, "Your dream. The turtle. The CD."

A man's sign says, "Down on luck. Can you spare any change. God bless."

Mrs. Norman says, "Oh, yes."

Mr. Norman says, "How did you get the CD out of the turtle?"

Curtis walks over to the other kid on the lawn. The kid's name is Lloyd and he lives five houses down and he's not really like the other kids. His front yard was once orange for a few days before the threatening letters, the midnight calls, the broken windows. It's green now.

Mrs. Norman says, "Oh, it was the darnedest thing. I had to take an ice pick and smash the turtle's shell."

Lloyd says, "Hi, Curtis."

Curtis says, "Hi, Lloyd."

Lloyd is pretending to jump rope. Occasionally the imaginary rope catches his foot and he says "darn" or "for Pete's sake" and he begins again. Lloyd says, "Do you have your passport ready?"

Curtis says, "I don't know."

Lloyd says, "My mother won't let me play Bear v. Shark."

Curtis says, "Everyone knows."

Lloyd says, "She thinks it's dumb and violent."

Curtis says, "It's just for fun."

Lloyd practices the fox-trot, smirking coyly at an invisible partner.

Curtis says, "Is she plotting its downfall?"

Lloyd says, "She's not plotting anything. She never comes outside anymore."

Curtis says, "Everyone knows."

Lloyd winks and says, "The pleasure is all mine."

Curtis says, "Is she crazy?"

Lloyd stops dancing. His small sneakers have too many stripes to be the right kind. *Way* too many. His shirt is terry cloth.

He says, "Maybe."

Matthew says, "Curtis, get over here and help."

Lloyd says, "My mom told me to come here and tell you to be careful."

Curtis says, "Me?"

Lloyd does a crisp cartwheel on the lawn, and then another one. He says, "Yes. She said to be very careful."

Matthew says, "Come *on,* butthole."

Curtis has been in and out of plenty of dangerous situations, and he's got the calluses on his gaming thumb to prove it. He says, "Nobody gets hurt in Bear v. Shark, Lloyd."

Lloyd does a magic trick and holds out his open hand to Curtis. There's a small glassy ball in his palm.

Curtis says, "At school, when our class voted. It was tied. Fourteen bear votes and fourteen shark votes."

Lloyd says, "Curtis, do you want my lucky marble?"

Curtis says, "But there are twenty-nine of us in class."

Lloyd says, "You should take it."

Curtis says, "You didn't vote, did you?"

Matthew throws a stick at Curtis.

Curtis says, "'Bye, Lloyd," and walks back to the driveway. The driveway is painted black.

Lloyd takes off toward home, on either a pretend horse or a pretend motorcycle.

Matthew says, "His mom is totally crazy."

Curtis says, "Hey Matt, what's a marble?"

17

The Last Folksinger

Meanwhile.

The Last Folksinger and the Last Folksinger's Dog climb into their beat-up van and point it toward Las Vegas. The Last Folksinger is tired.

His guitar says, "This machine kills fake animals."

While he drives, the Last Folksinger opens his fan mail.

One letter says, "If I were you, I wouldn't step one foot across the border, you pinko shithead."

Another letter in blue crayon says, "Your going to be dead fucker."

Woody's got his head out the window, he's licking the wind, ears pinned back, eyes all squinty.

Another letter says, "1. You are useless. 2. This is America. 3. I hate you."

The Last Folksinger closes the mailbag and takes a harmonica from his shirt pocket and plays "Rambling BvS Blues No. 8," one hand on the wheel.

The weigh station is closed, the left lane ends, the speeding fines are doubled in a work zone.

Woody turns three times on the ripped vinyl bench seat, sighs, and puts his big yellow Lab head on the Last Folksinger's lap. His brow looks kind of furrowed and worried the way a dog's can.

18

Scenic Bivouac

Mr. and Mrs. Norman checking the house one last time. Some of the little red lights are flashing and some are not. Everything seems OK.

What exactly are hatches and how does one batten them down?

A phone rings.

Hello.

Mr. Norman.

Yes.

How are you today?

I'm happy with my long-distance service.

And yet?

I'm afraid I have to go. I'm on my way out the door.

I know.

What?

Mr. Norman, you don't really care who wins, do you?

Who is this?

One of you.

I'm happy with my Internet service provider.

It's not really important, is it? The outcome.

Who is this? I've got to go.

Mr. Norman, have you ever heard of TeleTown?

Of course.

What do you know about it?

Everyone knows about TeleTown. It's the scenic bivouac featured on so many postcards and calendars and screensavers.

There's more.

Gypsies live there and make cookies. There are a million TVs, with more arriving all the time.

You don't know everything about TeleTown.

I don't really know what a bivouac is.

Just know that we're out here.

Who? Where? What are you selling?

Travel well.

Wait.

Yes?

Help me.

What?

I'm happy with my car insurance.

Good-bye.

Mrs. Norman says, "Who was that?"

Mr. Norman says, "A mysterious caller."

Mrs. Norman says, "Well what did they want?"

Mr. Norman says, "That is exactly what I don't know."

19

A Dead Mouse Is Still a Mouse

The Normans of America aren't even out of their suburban driveway when Curtis, the younger of the two boys, starts talking from the back of the Sport Utility Vehicle (SUV) about this couple that had a baby even though the woman had been in prison a long time but the husband had met her on a conjurer visit and they cut holes in their jeans and hid from the security cameras in the visiting room.

Mr. Norman (driving) says, "Jesus." He is mildly aroused. The part about the holes in the jeans.

Mrs. Norman (front, passenger side) says, "That's *conjugal* visit, Curtis."

Curtis says, "What did I say?"

Mr. Norman, neck cradled in the Vibra-Dream Plus, says, "You said jugular visit."

Curtis says, "Oh. Well that's what they said on the Television."

Mr. Norman says, "They said jugular visit on the Television?"

Curtis says, "Yeah, on the Prison Network."

Mr. Norman says, "Huh."

Mrs. Norman, feet resting flat on the floor shoulder width apart, says, "No, honey, you said *conjurer* visit."

Curtis says, "I could have sworn I said jugular."

Mrs. Norman says, "And I don't really want you talking about prison sex back there."

Somewhere nearby something explodes, rattling the futuristic cup holders in the Sport Utility Vehicle. Somewhere nearby someone screams.

Curtis says, "Well, that's just what they said on the Television."

Mr. Norman says, "Gosh, people do find a way, don't they?"

Mrs. Norman says, "Larry."

The Normans (husband and wife) have not slept in the same bed in some time. Mr. Norman sleeps not well. Mrs. Norman has turned to Posture. They met somewhere and they fell in love and they both just *knew* it was right and there were nights, weren't there nights?, all coiled up with their silly, tender jokes and their fingers tracing faces, the ruined sheets, the smell of their bodies, the ache and shimmer of the future, some clock somewhere chiming three, then four, on a weeknight. Curtis says something and then Matthew says something. There were nights, his lips on the pulse of her neck, whispering Sweetheart let's make love in every state of the union and Vegas, too. Sweetheart I want to memorize you.

It wasn't a movie. It may have happened. It wasn't a movie.

Mr. Norman drives the Sport Utility Vehicle through neighborhoods lined with splendid trees, their thick trunks columned in classical decay, their black, leafless branches like skeleton fingers reaching over the oily streets.

It always seemed like her hair, Mrs. Norman's hair, got curlier while she slept. In the morning a beautiful mess.

Mr. Norman says, "What kind of trees, boys?" A quiz.

The boys say, "Dead."

Mr. Norman says, "Aha, but a dead mouse is still a mouse."

Mrs. Norman says, "It's all this heat."

Mr. Norman says, "I thought it was all those chemicals in the ground."

Matthew says, "I thought it was Dutch lime disease."

Mrs. Norman says, "Well, yes, but it's the heat that makes the chemicals so bad. It's a symbiotic relationship."

She (the cordless vibrating pillow) says, "You, sir, are a fantastic driver."

Matthew says to Curtis (his younger brother), "*Conjurer* visit?"

Matthew says, "You a moron."

Curtis says, "You."

They met and fell in love. He had never seen anyone ski like that.

A woman skimming across the top of water will melt your heart. A woman with tan arms and her own life vest will make you forget all the others.

Matthew says, "You a dick sandwich."

Curtis says, "*You're* the dick sandwich."

Matthew says, "I don't need this from you, bear-hugger."

Mrs. Norman says, "It's penis, boys, and that's enough."

Matthew says, "You don't even have an idea what a penis sandwich is."

Curtis says, "I do, too."

Mr. Norman says, "Neither do I."

He (our hero) steers the burgundy Sport Utility Vehicle (SUV) around the entrance ramp and onto the freeway, weaving a slalom course around the scorched black husks of burned-out American sedans with power windows and antilock brakes.

The Normans are on their way.

20

Brainteaser

And now this . . .

Tom, just where did the Bear v. Shark mania originate?

Well, Mindy, a lot of ink and even some blood have been spilled trying to answer precisely that question. It just so happens that there is a bitter, long-standing, and litigious dispute involving the origins of America's favorite pastime.

Could you elaborate, Tom?

Sure, Mindy. In essence, some believe the Bear v. Shark question to be a very old one. Recently, a medievalist at Columbia produced a fragment of a text that he believes was written by a little-known French philosopher and theologian in the eleventh century. The author of the fragment is essentially scoffing at the intense debate generated over a question that is, he believes, a "no-brainer," to use the modern parleyvoo. Mindy, it appears this little French monk was quite the bear man!

(Mindy laughs. Her bone structure is exquisite. Her ex-boyfriend Nate lost big money on Bear v. Shark I.)

The text in translation reads, "And yet why is this a matter that must perplex us all so? The bear is angry and really strong. . . . The shark has enough teeth certainly for a single mouth, but in its fins we see frailty and, in essence, a smallness of spirit."

So, Tom, the question goes back at least to the Mid-Evil period.

Well, Mindy, there has been some doubt about the authenticity of the fragment. In fact, at the recent annual conference of a prominent scholarly organization, one speaker went so far as to publicly denounce the fragment as a hoax, which stirred up a bit of a fracas in the ivory tower. Mindy, according to one report, a retired Aquinas expert was inadvertently gouged in the eyeball during the scuffle.

That's interesting, Tom. Any other ideas about where this whole craze may have started?

As a matter of fact, Mindy, others have argued that Bear v. Shark is older yet, that it is, in essence, of ancient Eastern origin. Some would have it that Bear v. Shark is essentially a variation on a Buddhist koan, or a paradoxical riddle presented to Zen students to help them break free of reason and, in essence, achieve enlightenment.

Kind of like a brainteaser, Tom?

Essentially, yes. But while there is undoubtedly a beguiling, meditative, even spiritual quality to the question, there is also scant evidence that Bear v. Shark is Zen.

Well, then, Tom, what about Darwin's famous quip?

Mindy, experts can find no evidence to support the widely circulated story that Darwin once remarked to Huxley, "If the indolent and bumbling bear but put yet a scratch on the awful shark, I will verily eat my hat." In essence, the story appears to be made up.

So where does that leave us, Tom?

Well, folks who study the matter are essentially in agreement that the Bear v. Shark problem as it is now generally stated—"Who would win in a fight between a bear and a shark?"—is not ancient or medieval or even Victorian, but in fact dates back, in essence, no more than eight or ten years.

Is that right?

Ever since an enterprising young man named Elton Thigpen patented the Bear v. Shark question five years ago and then sold it to HardCorp for $11 million, no fewer than 250 people have come forward to claim that they were, in essence, the ones to invent the modern-day koan. Of these, some seventy-five have brought lawsuits.

Against Mr. Thigpen?

Essentially, yes, and also against HardCorp and each other.

I see. When will the madness end, Tom?

Well, Mindy, certainly not before the showdown on August eighteenth, when, as they say, the land will meet the sea in Las Vegas.

And is there any talk of a rubber match if the bear should win this time around, Tom?

Mindy, you can never rule out a rematch.

Thanks, Tom. Stay tuned, The Zinger's coming up with your weekend forecast, plus we'll catch you up to speed on that horrible passenger train disaster last night.

21

In the Lord
All Things Are Possible

The trip odometer says, "111," and the digital clock on the Sport Utility Vehicle dashboard says, "1:12."

I think you see the possibilities here.

Mr. Norman accelerates out of cruise control. He is searching for something real like when Mrs. Norman used to lick his teeth when they kissed. Was it his teeth? Was it her tongue? Was it on TV? Something got licked, something got bit. It was good and so long ago.

Mrs. Norman says, "What are you doing?"

Mr. Norman says, "I'm trying to get the trip odometer and the clock to match up." He says, "I think that would be neat."

Mrs. Norman says, "Neat?"

Mr. Norman says, "Pleasing." He keeps accelerating, swerving to the shoulders to pass slower cars, oil fires, dead dogs, hoboes. He says, "Meaningful."

The Vibra-Dream Plus says, "Yes. Oooh, yes."

Mrs. Norman tenses and her posture becomes even better than it had been before, and it had been very good. She says, "Well, we could just reset the clock to match the odometer."

This is Mr. Norman's life partner? Reset the clock and odometer? How does this come to be, this chasm, this gulf in sensibility? Could you even feel it if someone licked your teeth?

Mr. Norman says, "But then we wouldn't have earned it."

He jerks the wheel, pulling onto the dusty, sun-scorched median to pass a school bus with a shark painted the length of its side. The shark is wearing a purple satin robe with gold letters.

The satin robe says, "In the Lord all things are possible."

On the tail of the shark, some bearrorist has spray-painted, "FLUKE."

Mrs. Norman says, "Earned what?"

Mr. Norman, licking his top front teeth, says, "The meaning."

The trip odometer says, "112."

Mr. Norman says, "Hey, we did it. Look here, boys."

The boys (asleep) are asleep, wearing sunglasses and headphones. Matthew has a baseball hat on with triangular teeth on the bill and gill slits on the sides. That is one mean-looking cap.

The nine-inch Television (TV) is on the floor, pointed upward. The Extreme Weather Guy, a former war correspondent, says, "This is what the fog actually sees."

It's a safe bet that Matthew would have been nonchalant about his dad's feat. It might have reminded Curtis of something else really cool and recent.

The clock says, "1:13."

Mr. Norman says, "Shoot."

He slows down and resets the cruise control.

Mrs. Norman says, "But you did it, honey."

Mr. Norman says, "They did match up there for a few seconds."

Another fan letter in the bottom of the Last Folksinger's mailbag says, "If you think you were treated shabbily at BvS on Ice, just you wait."

Mrs. Norman says, "And you earned it, too."

Mr. Norman says, "Funny thing is, I still didn't feel much of anything."

22

The Old Televisions, Part III

People used to come home from a hard day's work and sit with bad posture in front of the Television and just flip and flip and flip. All night long, flipping past channels showing junk that they didn't want to watch. The remote. Some people say clicker. Some say driver or wand. At my house we said phaser. And sure, I remember a time when we changed those suckers *by hand.* They knew they were missing something. They wanted something better. Hundreds of channels, but most of them were unsuited for a specific viewer's quirky, eccentric individual tastes. They knew they wanted to be watching Television, but they weren't really enjoying it. Flip, flip, flip. Then along came ESP TV, the TV that knows you—*you*—the one that reads your mind. From a comprehensive main menu, you program up to 38 General Topics of Personal Interest (GTPI)—racket sports, vegetable gardening, medium-soft porn, antique road shows—and ESP TV shows you what you want to see. Don't like classic automobiles or starving African children? Well, you never have to see them again. Ever. Well, yes, and a patented sensor that *senses* when the viewer is bored or dissatisfied. Today's TVs flip themselves, move on, find the ideal programming and find it fast. Those old ESP TV infomercials are classics now, the woman in the sequined bikini smashing the remote control with a sledgehammer.

"The clicker, Roger, is a thing of the past, just like the waffle iron and the novel."

"And just like viewer dissatisfaction, Buzz!"

23

Ten-Second Debate

Mr. Norman drives. Las Vegas is still far away, the topless women, the cheap buffets, the hotel lobby aquariums, the happy songs of the slots. And the Bear and the Shark, realer than life, grappling while a nation holds its breath and its lottery tickets.

Neil Postman says, "Ignorance is always correctable. But what shall we do if we take ignorance to be knowledge?"

Everything will be fine. In Las Vegas, everything will be made right. The Spectacle transforms, it redeems.

Mr. Norman turns on the radio.

An FM (frequency modulation) gangster says, "My bitch left so fast she left skid marks."

Mr. Norman hits the scan button.

A trustworthy-sounding guy says, "If you're sick and tired of the nutbag babblers on those other stations, turn your dial to Smash 94, the babble-blockin' rocker. We don't talk, we just play the extreme light rock that we know you want to hear."

Mr. Norman hits the scan button.

An excited guy says, "Hernia Soda, for a taste so heavy, you'll need a spotter."

Mr. Norman hits the scan button.

The suspect's neighbor says, "He seemed like just a regular guy. He kept to himself, mostly."

Mr. Norman hits the AM (ante meridiem) button.

A crooner (old white guy) croons.

Mr. Norman hits the scan button.

A moderator says, "Welcome to Ten-Second Debate. Today's topic: abortion. The position of opening remark has been established by coin toss. Ready, debaters? OK . . . GO!"

A shaper of public opinion (Helen) says, "Freedom means choice, Rick."

A think tank member (Rick) says, "It's a child, not a choice, Helen."

Helen says, "If you can't trust me with a choice, etc., Rick."

Rick says, "Abortion, Helen, stops a beating heart."

Helen says, "Against abortion, Rick? Don't have one."

Rick says, "Helen, ever seen one of those little fetuses they suck out of there?"

The moderator rings a bell and says, "OK, there you have it. Our thanks to Rick Higgins and Helen Glass."

Helen says, "Rick, keep your laws off my body."

Mr. Norman can't quite figure out how he feels about abortion. There are so many different points of view.

Rick says, "Shut up, Helen."

Mr. Norman scans until he lands on Bear v. Shark: Talk Radio.

"Oh, I like this," Mrs. Norman says. "It's always so interesting."

Mr. Norman says, "It's a forum."

Mrs. Norman says, "It's the Greek ideal of participatory democracy."

Mr. Norman says, "Town meeting."

Mrs. Norman says, "Global village."

Mr. Norman says, "Fiber optics."

In the backseat, Curtis, the younger boy, a nice enough kid, shifts in his sleep and says, "Virtual summit."

24

Bear v. Shark: Talk Radio

The energetic, deep-voiced host of Bear v. Shark: Talk Radio says, "We're back and we have with us Dr. Sara Meredith, a professor of animal violence and habits, and the author of the controversial book *The Fin Factor*. Thanks for being here, Dr. Meredith."

Dr. Meredith says, "Thank you for having me, Wild Simon."

Wild Simon says, "Time for our next caller. This is Wayne in Roanoke, Virginia. Thanks for calling, Wayne. What's your question for Dr. Meredith?"

Wayne says, "I love your show, man."

Wild Simon says, "Thanks, Wayne."

Dr. Meredith says, "Hi, Wayne."

Wayne says, "Hi."

Wild Simon says, "Your question, Wayne?"

Wayne says, "I don't really have a question. I just wanted to say the shark is gonna kick *ass*."

Wild Simon says, "OK, thanks, Wayne."

Matthew says, "Which is what I've been saying for how long now?"

Wild Simon says, "Well, Dr. Meredith, isn't that pretty much what you're arguing in *The Fin Factor*?"

Dr. Meredith says, "In a small nutshell, yes."

Wild Simon says, "Because of the fins?"

Dr. Meredith says, "What?"

Wild Simon says, "The shark will win because of the fins?"

Dr. Meredith says, "Yes. It's my thinking that entirely too much attention has been paid to the teeth."

Mrs. Norman visualizes her spine as a tree trunk, like they say to.

Wild Simon says, "There are many rows and they are very sharp. When one falls out, two more grow back. They cut right through bone and metal."

Dr. Meredith sighs. She says, "Right."

Wild Simon says, "Doesn't 'fin' mean something in French?"

Dr. Meredith says, "Yes."

Wild Simon says, "What do you make of that?"

Dr. Meredith says, "I haven't really thought much about it."

Wild Simon says, "OK, this is Tina in The Bronx. You're on, Tina."

Tina says, "Our English word *berserk* comes from the ancient Scandinavian belief that if a warrior put on a bearskin shirt, called a bear-sark, that had been covered in oils and herbs, he would take on the power of the bear. It is said that these Viking warriors became frenzied and could literally eat through their enemy's armor and also they could catch on fire and not really be harmed much."

Wild Simon says, "Tina, do you have a question for Dr. Meredith?"

Wild Simon says, "Tina?"

Mr. Norman feels happy. Not happy, exactly, but safe and warm and drowsy. The warm, safe lull of the voices.

Wild Simon says, "Dr. Meredith, I heard somewhere that you've had death threats."

Dr. Meredith says, "Yes, that's true."

Wild Simon says, "Well, it could be worse, people could be indifferent."

Dr. Meredith says, "I guess so."

Wild Simon says, "You know, there was this great race car driver, Richard Petty or somebody, and the fans were getting on him, you know? The race fans were booing him good, and a reporter or someone asked Petty or whoever, you know, does all that booing ever bother you? And you know what he said?"

Dr. Meredith says, "Is Richard Petty still racing?"

Wild Simon says, "He said, 'Hey, at least they're making noise.'"

Dr. Meredith says, "Noise is never bad."

Wild Simon says, "Are these threats from bear people?"

Dr. Meredith says, "Yes, and from some shark people who don't think fins are all that important."

Wild Simon says, "It's a crazy world out there."

Dr. Meredith (author of *The Fin Factor*) says, "Most of the people I've met have been lovely."

Wild Simon says, "Time for one more caller. This is our old friend Dale in Houston. Hi, Dale. Welcome back. What's your question for Dr. Meredith?"

Dale says, "Hello?"

Wild Simon says, "You're on, Dale. Twenty seconds left."

Dr. Meredith says, "Hi, Dale."

Curtis says, "Houston is *windier* than so-called Chicago."

Dale says, "People root for the bear because it looks like us. It has ears and arms and eyes. The whole bear faction is just ethnocentric because bears are like humans. We're both vertebrates."

Dr. Meredith says, "Sharks are vertebrates, too, Dale."

Dale (in Houston) says, "Well, we're both mammals."

Wild Simon says, "Isn't a shark a mammal, too?"

Dr. Meredith says, "You're thinking of bats."

Dale says, "A shark's not a mammal because it doesn't have a pouch or hairy young."

Wild Simon says, "Dale, do you have a question for Dr. Meredith?"

Dale says, "I'd like to say hi to Rusty and Bingo in Galveston."

Wild Simon says, "Thanks for calling, Dale."

Matthew says, "It's like I *hate* Dale."

Dr. Meredith says, "'Bye, Dale."

25

Dutch Treat

Is Dutch elm disease technically Dutch?

What do you mean by technically?

Is the elm Dutch or the disease or both?

It's an example of what they refer to essentially as an unclear moderator.

Like large animal clinic?

Like dirty book publisher.

Like small Television room?

Like red wine glass.

Like thick juicy steaks?

No.

What about Dutch uncle?

You can't say Dutch uncle anymore. That's like calling somebody a dwarf. They like to be called little people.

Dutch uncles want to be called little people?

You can't say Dutch courage anymore either because that's offensive to drunk people.

How about Dutch oven?

That's OK.

Dutch door?

Fine.

Dutch Guiana?

We say Suriname now.

Dutch cheese, Dutch auction, Dutch clover, Dutchman's breeches, Dutch Colonial?

All OK.

Dutch treat?

Oh the flaming dessert.

No you're thinking of bananas Florentine.

26

The Cockfights Ain't Pipin'

A public service announcement (PSA) from Jasper Palace, the voice of Uncle Jaws on the Tuesday-night situational comedy *The Sharkleys*:

Rise up, Jasp Palace here, and this is a big bullhorn to all the preadults out there. Hey, we all know how much funny fun bears and sharks are, right? Jam on toast, mes enfants!

But hear me out, you teen machines, there is a flip to the up. A bear or a shark can also be a very serious and even life-threatening matter. Last year alone, sixteen people were killed—that's sixteen corpsy corpses, my deputy dogs—dozens were injured, and hundreds more were arrested when they tried to take American-style fun and entertainment into their own felonious, no-thinkin' hands.

Use your lobe, kids. Leave the Bear v. Shark scrap to the computer tie-guys. If someone you know wants to get hold of one of these beasty beasts or arrange a real fight, just walk away. Show 'em your bakery! See, the cockfights ain't pipin'. And parents, it's never too early to talk to your kids about the dangers of obtaining live bears and sharks, or pitting them against each other in a real duel. Zip, let's keep Bear v. Shark safe, fun, and lawful. *Yes, ma'am.*

Fricky-frack, hypes. See you on Tuesday nights.

27

Planet Peanut Brittle

Don't forget about the Normans.

They're taking a trip to Las Vegas. They're making good time, too, by the looks of the billboards and retail centers whizzing past. Sometimes you have to tear down a big store and put a bigger one where the big one used to be. The bigger store holds more stuff.

The family has traveled 194 American miles and Mr. Norman knows it.

A billboard says, "Exit now for Planet Peanut Brittle." There is a picture of a guy in a space suit walking across lumpy brown candy, giving a thumbs-up to Mission Control. The image is somehow both futuristic and nostalgic. Janus-faced: It's the sticky treat for the new millennium, but it's also the irresistible snack you remember as a child. The aftertaste of time. Our special ingredient is memory. Those PR wizards, they've done what nobody thought they could do: they've dusted off peanut brittle, updated it, refurbished it, made it appropriate for today's hectic world. It's not your granny's recipe. It's PB2K. They've made peanut brittle timeless, cross-generational. Peanut brittle is back, more relevant than ever, exit *now*.

Mr. Norman exits. It's good to be spontaneous on a trip.

Mrs. Norman is playing an electronic knitting game. The way you win is to make a scarf or an afghan or a turtleneck sweater, except it's not a real sweater you can wear. There is a cross-stitch cartridge, too. And one called *Darning Mania!*

Mrs. Norman says, "Where are you going?"

Brittle sticks, brittle logs, brittle rings.

Mr. Norman says, "I thought we'd get some peanut brittle."

Matthew says, "What I'm saying is just try getting it out of your bicuspids."

Mrs. Norman looks up from her knitting game. She's on Mittens Level. There is the sound of a clock and then the sound of smashing glass. Game over. With knitting, you hesitate, you die.

Mrs. Norman says, "Larry, you know I'm allergic to peanut brittle. It makes my tongue swell up."

Mr. Norman says, "What?"

Mrs. Norman says, "You know that."

Mr. Norman parks the SUV in the spacious parking lot of Planet Peanut Brittle. There's a guy with a fin taped to his back handing out coupons.

Mr. Norman says, "Well, we'll get the kind without peanuts."

Mrs. Norman says, "No, it's the brittle that makes me so sick. I'm allergic to the brittle. I'm fine with peanuts."

Mr. Norman turns off the car but keeps both hands on the wheel. He's staring straight ahead. Sometimes he gets so tired.

He says, "You've always been allergic?"

Mrs. Norman says, "Something in the brittle. My tongue just fills my mouth."

Curtis says, "Let's see, Mom."

Mrs. Norman says, "It was a nice thought, though."

It's brittle-rific.

Mrs. Norman says, "Let's go ahead and get some lunch while we're stopped."

Matthew says, "Hey, how many bears does it take to screw in a lightbulb?"

Was Mrs. Norman a graceful water skier? Where is her birthmark and what is its shape? What really funny thing did she do when she was five? Does she like the pulp in her orange juice? Where was the honeymoon? What is the feel of your naked belly pressed against someone else's? Quick, what grade is Matthew in? How is Curtis doing in school? Do the other kids like him? Just who *are* these people in the car with Mr. Norman and what makes their tongues swell?

It's 618 miles to Las Vegas, but then what? A bear, a shark, a level playing field.

Mr. Norman rests his head on the steering wheel.

He says, "Five."

28

Darwin Dome

Here's what happened, essentially:

HardCorp told Las Vegas that if the city didn't build a 65,000-seat arena for "Bear v. Shark II: Red in Tooth and Claw," the big show would move elsewhere. The corporation had gotten plenty of nice offers from other cities, including Los Angeles and Buffalo and Miami.

Vegas officials crunched the numbers and figured out that the city could tear down three casinos, build the Darwin Dome for the big event, then tear down the dome and rebuild the casinos, and still come out in the black.

Done deal, technically.

The best tickets went to executives, politicians, military officers, movie stars, professional athletes and wrestlers, TV personalities, foreign dignitaries, puppet despots, models, gangsters, and game show hosts.

Fifteen thousand tickets were available through a lottery. Over 21 million (21,000,000) people entered the lottery, and the lucky winners were given the opportunity to buy two tickets for $2,500 each.

A handful of tickets were given away in Specially Marked Boxes of Sea-n-Lea Meat Snacks, void where prohibited, check package for details.

And four tickets were given to the family of the winner of a national essay contest open to elementary school students. Students were to write a 250-word response to the question, "What does Bear v. Shark mean to America?"

Curtis Norman of America, who had gotten chubby on Sea-n-Lea Meat Snacks, won the essay contest.

29

Some Jokes

How many bears does it take to screw in a lightbulb?

How many?

Five. One to screw in the bulb and four to pick sharks' teeth out of their asses.

Knock, knock.

Who's there?

Bear.

Bear who?

Bear with me while I kick this shark's ass.

An invisible bear goes to see the doctor and sits in the waiting room.

The receptionist, who just happens to be a shark, says to the invisible bear, "I'm sorry, the doctor can't see you right now."

Why did the chicken cross the road?

To get a better look at the [*bear* or *shark*] ripping off the [*shark's* or *bear's*] head and feasting on its entrails.

Hey, do you know what they used to call the Internet when it first became available?

I give up.

Get this: The *Information Superhighway*.

30

Ethos

The sign says, "Ma's Old-Fashioned Interstate Tavern."

Another sign says, "Bear and Shark lottery tickets sold here."

Another sign says, "If you can bearly stand the heat, then shark your car and come on in!"

Mrs. Norman says, "This looks good."

The hostess says, "Four for lunch?"

She (the hostess) says, "Smoking or nonsmoking?"

She says, "Internet access?"

The Normans follow the paw prints on the tile floor to their booth. Mr. Norman wonders what might be the best way to kill yourself. He saw it on a Television program. It was a contest.

Mrs. Norman asks the waitress if Ma's Old-Fashioned Interstate Tavern BearBurger is really made out of bear or if that's just a cute name like the Sharka Colada.

The waitress says, "I'll go check."

A pop singer says, "Baby baby baby baby."

Thoreau says, "We are in great haste to construct a magnetic telegraph from Maine to Texas;"

There is a Television mounted to the wall above the Normans' booth. A reporter is on some busy city street, interviewing passersby. It might be New Orleans, maybe Lansing.

Matthew plays handheld Bear Killer. The game says, "Beep, beep. Grrrrrr."

He (Matthew) says, "I saw on the Internet that people get *real* bears and sharks to fight."

Mrs. Norman says, "Yes, I read about that. They're called cock-fights."

Curtis, the youngest boy, raised on sugar substitute and embedded chips and digital enhancement, says, "What?"

Mrs. Norman says, "They're called that because male sharks and male bears are known as cocks."

Curtis says, "What do they call the women?"

Mr. Norman stares at the Television. You could jump off something high, for instance. He says, "They say the shark almost always wins."

Matthew pokes Curtis in the neck. He says, "See."

Curtis says, "Ow."

The pop singer says, "Oooh yeah, don't you feel it, baby?"

The waitress says, "It's just a normal hamburger."

Mrs. Norman says, "So it's made from a cow?"

The waitress, who sometimes cries for no apparent reason and who answers "strongly agree" to the question, often posed on psychological evaluations, "Do you often have feelings of despair and hopelessness?," says, "I'll go check."

Bear Killer says, "Tick tick tick tick." Time is running out. See, if you don't find the bear den, infiltrate it, and kill all three cubs with a big rock in a certain amount of time, the mother bear comes home and gores you with a halberd.

The guy in the booth next to the Normans says, "I saw one cockfight Web site that said the bear picked up the shark over his head and threw it into the audience, injuring five."

Curtis says, "Fricky-frack, hypes."

Matthew says, "Yeah, but that same Web site also said that the bear shouted, 'I vanquish thee,' as he threw the shark which I doubt very seriously he did."

Thoreau says, "but Maine and Texas, it may be, have nothing important to communicate."

Mr. Norman looks down from the Television at the guy in the next booth over. The guy's eyes look funny. The guy keeps glancing at Mr. Norman and making quick jerking motions with his head. Toward something, the dessert case or the rest rooms or the Zoloft Smoothie Kiosk (ZSK).

Curtis says, "The Internet raises some thorny issues about credibility and ethos."

Everyone looks at Curtis, this preadult, this virtual madman. At his Keyboard he has taken countless lives, ain't no thing, he has received outrageous sexual favors from CyberWhores with tits out to here, digital fucking machines born to pleasure Curtis Norman.

Matthew (to Curtis) says, "Shut *up*, fag."

Mr. Norman knows that you would want to wait until after Bear v. Shark II, of course. You could electrocute yourself easily enough, it seems. There's electricity everywhere.

A woman on the Television clutching a bag of groceries tells the reporter that sharks are, like, 90 percent teeth.

Curtis says, "It was on the Internet. Some professor had a Web site. He turned out not to be a professor, just a fisherman who reads a lot, but I think his point about ethos still holds."

The waitress says, "It's mostly cow."

The Normans order BearBurgers. And Sharky Temples for the kids.

Curtis says, "Can you pass the sugar substitute?"

A guy on the Television wearing a bike helmet and a blood-soaked shirt says that bears are as fast as cougars.

Matthew says, "What you have to remember is that a person who reads the Sunday *New York Times* gets more information than a French villager in the eighteenth century got in his whole lifetime."

Mrs. Norman says, "*Their* whole lifetime."

The head-jerking funny-eyed guy in the next booth says, "Yes, but people are living longer now."

Mr. Norman, there was always carbon monoxide, says, "Where did you hear that information?"

Matthew says, "Some show on French villagers. Turns out they had real problems with gum disease."

Mrs. Norman says, "The way I heard it was that a person who habitually reads newspapers knows more, in essence, than an eighteenth-century French person."

Curtis says, "The point is that it's hard to know what to believe."

Matthew says, "No, the point is that there is a lot of stuff to believe."

Mr. Norman says, "Isn't the point that you shouldn't believe anything?"

The waitress says, "Aren't those all the same point?"

The reporter on the Television says, "Back to you, Derek."

31

Bear v. Shark: The Essay

A REASON TO LIVE

(by Curtis Norman)

In today's society there is a lot of bad news. Just for an example of this is tornadoes, assassinations, tainted food, and killer bees. Other examples are pollution, bad roads, heroin, teen pregnancy, and rabies. These problems aren't anyone's fault, most of them (like killer bees) are natural and can't be controlled by human destiny.

It can be difficult to be happy with all this bad news around. For instance, people are grumpy and many of them commit suicide. Men tend to choose guns and women choose pills. I say choose life!

Bear v. Shark allows people to forget about their own problems and the troubles in the world and just be happy. Bear v. Shark gives people a reason to be excited about their day. Instead of sad about gang violence or a collapsing infrastructure people can be upbeat because they are happy. Their minds are on something else. Say, which side are you on? Are you for the bear or the shark? And what about those fins anyway?

In closing, my gardener is Dutch and he doesn't have a culture. But America is great because it has a culture and Bear v. Shark helps us have a culture.

32

The Fur Team

The guy in the booth next to the Normans, the guy looking at Mr. Norman in a strange manner, eventually joins the family for lunch. He squeezes in beside the boys. He's wearing an old faded black "Bear v. Shark I" T-shirt from the first event two years earlier.

It (the shirt) looks like a classic. It looks authentic, though they sell them like that now, faded and threadbare. They do a nice job. It's really hard to tell.

Curtis notices the shirt. He says, "Were you there?"

The guy nods. He says, "Third row. My uncle worked on the bear programming team. He hooked me up with the tickets."

Curtis says, "Too bad about what happened."

The guy says, "Yeah."

Curtis says, "Was the bear's head really that small?"

Mrs. Norman says, "Curtis."

The guy says, "No, it's OK."

Curtis says, "I read on the Internet that the Internet photos of the tiny head are an Internet hoax."

The guy says, "I read that too, but I was there and I have to say, the bear's head was pretty small."

Matthew says, "Did your uncle hook you up again this time?"

Mrs. Norman says, "Matthew."

The guy says, "He got fired. HardCorp fired all the bear programming personnel, even though my uncle just worked on the fur team. That's all he did, fur."

Matthew says, "The fur looked a little patchy."

Mr. Norman says, "Why is it that we can send a bear and a shark to the moon, but we can't make a good razor for sensitive skin?"

Curtis says, "Do you have a Web site?"

Mrs. Norman says, "They did the right thing by just starting it all over again. Plus, it's just so fun to have something to look forward to."

The crackling intercom says, "Has anyone lost a baby? There's a tiny baby up here."

A pop singer says, "Oh my sweet angel, I can't live without you."

Mrs. Norman says, "It's the anticipation more than anything."

The guy says, "Listen, I'm not saying a normal-headed bear could take a shark, but this was just no contest."

Mrs. Norman says, "What does he do now?"

The guy is kicking Mr. Norman under the table. He says, "What?"

Mrs. Norman says, "Your uncle, what does he do now?"

The pop singer promises to kill his sweet angel's husband.

The guy says, "Oh, he shot himself."

33

Patents Pending

Possum v. Squirrel
Owl v. Deer
Squid v. Monkey
Cow v. Mastiff
Varmint v. Critter
Scorpion v. Pigeon
Blind v. Deaf
Jew v. Puerto Rican
Manx v. Mutt
Spanish Moss v. Kudzu
Hitler v. Elvis
Toddler v. Snake
Middle Manager v. Homeless
Oliver Wendell v. Sherlock

34

A Shark Never Sleeps

The guy from the other booth finishes his Shark Blood Soup, which is really a nice tomato basil.

The crackling intercom says, "People, please check around your table to make sure you have not lost a baby."

Through the tavern's TV-screen-shaped windows Mr. Norman can see the ceaseless interstate traffic, the Median Police with their lightning guns and their caged truck overflowing with hoboes. He can see the migrant workers putting up new billboards, the airbrushed women and their cleavage and their sexy shampoos, their sexy bug sprays, their sexy canned meat products for families on the go, who has time to cook these days, tastes like fresh meat, I couldn't tell the difference, you won me over, I'll try it.

The waitress, who, yes, often has trouble sleeping, says, "Can I bring you all anything else?"

On the Television an angry and tattered man with no good connections, no stock portfolio, no health insurance, no Internet provider, no sense of common decency, no chance of ever making sweet hot virtual love to the likes of the airbrushed hucksters who haunt the modern interstate, says to the reporter, "What?"

The reporter (nose job, bulletproof jacket) says, "Sir, who do *you* think would win in a fight between a bear and a shark?"

The angry tattered man says, "A shark never sleeps."

He gets up in the reporter's face. He jabs a greasy finger in the reporter's chest. He says, "If the shark sleeps, it will drown."

Curtis says, "Advantage: Bear."

The waitress says, "Some coffee or dessert?"

The guy says, "Not so fast, little camper."

Curtis says, "The shark never sleeps. So it must be tired and groggy. Think about how you feel if you haven't had any sleep."

The guy is trying to pass a napkin note to Mr. Norman. He says, "I'm not sure I see what you're driving at."

Matthew says, "But bears sleep half the year."

The guy says, "That's true."

The waitress says, "Leave room for cream?"

Curtis says, "Exactly. The bear burrows into the soft clay and hibernates during the winter months. Thus when he is awake and fighting sharks, his temperament is strong and well rested."

Mrs. Norman says, "*Their* temperament." It is difficult to sit well in the booth's squishy seat. Difficult, not impossible.

The guy from the other booth, the jerky one with the urgent secret napkin note, says, "I'm starting to see how it all comes together."

Curtis smiles and does a little dance in the booth.

Matthew says, "Hold everything. Thomas Edison didn't need any sleep."

The guy from the other booth says, "Well, how about that? I guess I knew about the ponytail and the spectacles—well, and the kite, of course—but the insomnia is a new one for me."

A cute little red-haired girl is ogling pies in the dessert case. Her shirt says, "You ever seen a *shark* in a circus?"

Mrs. Norman says, "Is it technically insomnia if you don't need the sleep?"

The guy says, "What do you mean by technically?"

Mr. Norman gazes out the smog-stained Television windows at the interstate, where a team of migrant workers is now installing a billboard featuring a picture of Jesus on the cross. Looks like maybe Jesus has a personal trainer. The hues are sexy, the composition is avant-garde. Jesus has nice pecs, a strong chin, a swarthy complexion. The billboard says, "Jesus loves the Truth and hates litter."

The crackling intercom describes the baby as bald and dirty. Tiny overalls. It's just a matter of coming to the register to claim the baby.

The waitress says, "Insomnia sort of implies you're trying to sleep but can't."

The guy says, "But you can be hungry and not eat, can't you?"

The waitress says, "Yes, you can."

Mr. Norman says, "Thomas Edison said, 'Hey, Watson, come here I need you.'"

Mrs. Norman says, "No, honey, I think you're thinking of Alexander Lloyd Webber."

Matthew says, "Edison never slept and he invented electricity. Lack of sleep shows a certain resolve and strength of constitution, whereas hibernation indicates a slothful and indolent nature."

The guy from the other booth says, "Well, now, I knew the little man's argument was not airtight, though I could not quite find the flaw in it myself."

The secret note says, *You are not alone. There are others like you. If you keep your eyes open you will find us.*

The waitress says, "How about a Bear Claw or a CubCake?"

Curtis says, "A bear would rip Thomas Edison to shreds."

The baby just sits between the mints and the toothpicks, worried.

35

Oliver Wendell
v.
Sherlock

Watson was Frank Lloyd Wright's assistant?

If I was Watson, I'd just tell Sherlock if he needs me so bad, he can come in here. Fricky-frack, I'm busy with my own projects.

Who would win in a fight between Oliver Wendell Holmes and Sherlock Holmes?

Would both of them have normal-size heads?

Yes.

No outside help from assistants?

No.

No hidden weapons? They both wore those kind of long, flowy outfits.

No.

Sherlock, then.

I disagree. I think Ollie would unleash some wicked justice on that fictional sleuth.

Hey, who did Igor assist?

Wittgenstein.

Most people think that Wittgenstein is the name of the monster, but if you read the original translation, Wittgenstein is actually the name of the doctor.

What was the monster's name?

Tonto means stupid.

They say Lindbergh had an assistant.

36

The Shark's Erogenous Zone

Mr. Norman is not fully attuned to the conversation or the booth Television or the red-haired little girl's shirt (the back of which says, "Shut your big fat bear trap") or even the sexy clever billboards outside his Television-screen-shaped window.

Mr. Norman is thinking about having sex with a shark. Listen, not in an indecent or bestial way. Not at all. In Mr. Norman's mind it is tender lovemaking—respectful, consensual, aquatic. He imagines the tough rubbery feel of the scaleless skin. He imagines a wordless embrace. He imagines stroking the fins and gently tonguing the gill slits, which he imagines to be the shark's erogenous zone. The warm salt water laps against their bodies.

Seaweed, coral, Spanish galleons, glittering doubloons.

The shark arches its back, moans through razor teeth.

This is not filthy. This is genuine and beautiful, but Mr. Norman knows that nobody would understand.

How could they?

37

www.lindberghhoax.com

Greetings, Net nomads and nonbelievers. You are perhaps weary and full of misgiving and your road has been arid and unlined with fruit or stags. At this point you require the hearty, salty dinner of warriors. The dogma is like so much plankton for the likes of us! You need the bloody meat of TRUTH!

Take heart in that you have found for the moment a haven and a sanctuary on your arid travels. The very fact that you're here is a solid indicator that your mind is unfettered by the dross and shale emitted like so many pretty little sparks from our major media outlets. You refuse to simply swallow the party line and masticate the sweet candy that our "government" gives us. Good for you. The likes of such as you are a dwindling breed of nomads in the arid world and you are to be commended.

Now on to the substance of our meal. Below are some of the major facts in this case, any one of which would cast grave shadows of unreliability on this "solo flight" across the "Atlantic," but taken altogether they fairly shatter the myth like so many shattered eggs.

FACT: Records show that the *Spirit of Enola Gay*, the "plane" that "Lindbergh" supposedly used, was not registered with the U.S. Bureau of Aviation in 1927. It is as if the flying machine didn't even exist!

FACT: Recently declassified Soviet spy satellite photographs reveal that "Lindbergh" took a shortcut and never actually crossed the "Atlantic." What he may in fact have crossed is part of Canada and the Baltic Sea, a feat which had been done before.

FACT: In 1952, a Dutch woman came forward and said that she was on board the *Spirit of Enola Gay,* which severely calls into question the "solo" aspect of the "flight."

FACT: There's no way you can have enough fuel for that.

FACT: Just when this case was about to be blown open by unfettered investigators in an arid world, that's when the whole "kidnapping" thing with the "baby" happened, thus projecting a large smoke screen over the dubious feat.

Safe travels, Net nomads. Remember: In the arid world a traveler needs more substance than the opium of so-called "bears" and "sharks," the corporate tools that confuse and distract us from the TRUTH.

38

The Catch of the Day

The guy from the next booth over walks the Normans out to their Sport Utility Vehicle in the parking lot of Ma's Old-Fashioned Interstate Tavern.

Choppers say, "Buzz."

He says, "Gosh, it's been real nice getting to know you all."

Curtis says, "Likewise."

The guy says to Mrs. Norman, "You have a nice family. Those kids are sharp."

Mrs. Norman says, "Thank you. The school says they're just average, but I've always suspected they are gifted and talented."

Mr. Norman unlocks the Sport Utility Vehicle and gets in the driver's side. He's still thinking about making love to the shark. He thinks it might make a good cable TV movie, sort of a they-came-from-different-worlds thing.

The guy says, "They say the computer shark and bear are more real than real ones."

Curtis says, "Yeah, more lifelike."

Mr. Norman starts the Sport Utility Vehicle. He thinks it could be called *The Catch of the Day* or something clever like that. And maybe the shark's baby would get switched with another baby. Or maybe a human woman would agree to have the shark's baby but when it came time to deliver she just couldn't stand to give it up.

Mrs. Norman says, "Apparently they're just like a bear and shark, except even more so."

Matthew says, "Yeah, but let's not forget the first time around."

There would be a court scene. The lawyers would say the shark was unfit to be a mother. Witnesses would get badgered. There would be a lot of objecting. Your Honor, I don't really see how that's relevant here! That stern guy who plays Turk on *Bear Beach* could play the judge. Some objections would be sustained and others would be overruled.

Curtis says, "That was human error."

Matthew says, "Still."

The guy says, "They say they've got it all worked out now."

A policeman with a stun gun jerks a half-naked guy out of the dumpster in the parking lot. He (the policeman) says, "I wouldn't try any cowboy shit, mister."

Mrs. Norman has her hand on the handle of the passenger side door. Matthew and Curtis lean against the Sport Utility Vehicle. The guy from the next booth over rocks from one foot to the other.

The guy twitches and rubs his palms on his pants.

The ending would be sad, probably, but also laced with hope and redemption. Mr. Norman thinks maybe he could serve as an adviser on the film.

Mrs. Norman says, "Well."

The guy says, "It was really great spending time with you."

Mrs. Norman says, "OK, boys, let's get this show back on the road."

The guy says, "Let's keep in touch."

Matthew and Curtis climb into the Sport Utility Vehicle and put on their safety belts and headphones. Mrs. Norman sits in the passenger seat, shuts her door, and rolls down her window. She says, "You take care."

The guy says, "Thanks for the CubCake." He walks over to the driver's side and taps on the window. Mr. Norman rolls down the window. The guy says, "Drive safely." He (the guy) sticks his hand into the SUV and when Mr. Norman shakes the guy's hand, a note falls into his lap.

Mr. Norman says, "Thanks."

The note says, *We can help you.*

Mr. Norman pulls the Sport Utility Vehicle out of the parking lot. The kids and Mrs. Norman wave to the guy and the guy waves back.

Plaintiff, closing arguments, plea bargain.

Mrs. Norman says, "He sure was nice."

Mr. Norman says, "Your witness, Steve."

39

Pseudo-Context

OK, hands on your buzzers.

A: In his long-out-of-print book *Amusing Ourselves to Death: Public Discourse in the Age of Show Business,* this shrill cultural critic wrote, "A **pseudo-context** is a structure invented to give fragmented and irrelevant information a seeming use. But the use the pseudo-context provides is not action, or problem-solving, or change. It is the only use left for information with no genuine connection to our lives. And that, of course, is to amuse."

Q: Who is Neil Postman.

40

Bear v. Shark I: An Insider's Story

An excerpt from *Swimming with the Sharks: My Two Years at Hard-Corp,* by Alex Reid, as told to Wendy Timlin:

Of course, people will just remember the bear's head, which is a terrible shame because we gave the world a miracle that night in Los Angeles. People in my generation never dreamed that they'd see a real fight between a bear and a shark. There have always been cock fights, of course, but I'm talking about the real thing—computer-generated, three-dimensional projection. I'm talking about action so lifelike, so realistic, that it makes real bears and sharks look like cartoons.

For years, Bear v. Shark was just a speculative question, and people thought it would remain that way for a long time. "Who would win in a fight between a bear and a shark?" was no different than "How many angels would fit on the head of a pin?" or "What is the sound of one hand clapping?" or "Who was the better president, Martin Van Buren or William Howard Taft?" But we caught up to it. We tracked it down. We used technology to transform an intractable Zen-like riddle into a spectacle, an event, an experiment—something you could see, hear, and bet money on. This was magic. This was science and technology at their best, utilizing knowledge and equipment to solve problems that once seemed insoluble.

But we rushed it, we got greedy. We got intoxicated by our own power. A week before the show I knew we weren't ready, and I told my supervisor, Mr. B., but he said there was no turning back now, and I suppose he was right. None of us slept for days. We had a dress rehearsal, a simulation duel, in a secret underground site in New Mexico. Our natural setting was perfect, evocative of both beach and national park. And the animals looked fantastic. Their teeth needed to be whitened even more, but they were beautiful, and we all felt like gods. But we were brought back down to earth pretty quickly when the bear and the shark wouldn't fight. They "refused to engage," as the corporate memos said later. We waited and waited, but nothing ever happened. It's like they didn't even notice each other. After three hours, we shrank our setting by half, hoping to force an encounter, but those animals just had no interest in fighting. When the bear fell asleep and the shark lunged at one of the stage-hands, we called the thing off and started emergency planning.

We had six days until the show. We pulled all of our programmers off the Van Buren v. Taft project to help us out. But there are millions of lines of code and they are all strung together, tangled in a Gordian knot. When you start messing with code, you alter everything. As we used to say, when you change the paw, you change the claw. So we got them ready to fight, but the bear's head was altered in the process. It was minimized, as we programmers say. It was minimized by about 40 percent and I know people were upset, but honestly, when the lights went down and the music came on, we didn't know if the bear would even have a head or if we'd have a hairy shark or what.

We gave the people a miracle. We gave them magic. We gave them fourteen electrifying seconds, and I for one am not ashamed of that.

41

A Sage and Beneficent Despot

Out on the interstate.

The dashboard of the Normans' Sport Utility Vehicle (SUV) says, "Forget your worries, everything is fine."

The dashboard says, "You just leave everything to me."

It (this award-winning, first-in-its-class dashboard) says, "Listen, don't fight it. Look at me. Look at me, surrender yourself, we'll all live forever."

This dashboard does not tolerate anxiety or cynicism or ambiguity in the cockpit. Does not allow it. Transforms it with the stare of 100 beguiling eyes: the gauges, dials, and meters. Melts it with decimal-point precision, an unflagging vigilance, a terrifying will to power, and an ever-appropriate use of Light: crisp and bright and heedful of automotive risk where such prudence is called for, subtle and soulful elsewhere.

This is Warm Science—hard data and soft, Scandinavian design.

This dashboard forever changes the way you think about dashboards. This dashboard, in consumer tests, is consistently rated "the most trustworthy dashboard on the market."

The dashboard says, "Everything is as it should be," and the dashboard is *right*.

The meters, in earnest resolve, carry on their quiet rivalry (speedo v. odo, thermo v. tacho), each made better, more precise, through the crucible of healthy competition. Each device respects but does not fear the others. Each device is just happy to be there, just wants to make the most of the opportunity, just wants to thank the Lord for its God-given abilities.

The gas gauge verifies that the vehicle's barrel-chested fuel tank is, how shall we say, *nearly full*. The oil pressure gauge is quick to point out that the oil pressure is remarkably normal. The thermometers gather data at three different sites: outside the vehicle it is Hot (97 degrees); inside the vehicle it is Comfortable (73 degrees); the engine? Well, the engine is running royal-blue cool, no problem there.

This dashboard knows the way to Las Vegas.

The battery is charged, the headlights are on, the time is 3:38 P.M. PST (Pacific Standard Time), the speed is 74 miles per hour, the four-wheel drive is off (but ready to be on), the air conditioner is on (but ready, whenever called upon, to be off).

That orange light there means the tires are unlikely to explode.

This dashboard knows: twenty-four grains to a pennyweight, three scruples to a dram, twenty quires to a ream. A hogshead is two barrels and a township is thirty-six square miles, you got to get up pretty early in the morning to put one over on the dash.

The phone, the map, the CD player, the cruise control—like the very best waiters or retail store employees, these devices do not hassle or cloy, but are immediately available if their services are required.

Mrs. Norman says, "We are going to witness history this weekend."

Mr. Norman feels loose in the limbs. He believes that the dashboard is a sage and beneficent despot. Sure, there are sacrifices, but doesn't one always have to give up a little freedom to achieve stability and happiness?

Mr. Norman, his speech a bit slurred, says, "History."

Mrs. Norman says, "And it's something we'll all share. It's something we can pass on to our children and grandchildren."

Matthew says, "It's not like it won't be out on DVD in a month."

The dashboard says the windshield wiper fluid is almost precisely at the Manufacturer's Recommended Level.

42

The Most Recent Polls

- The majority (52 percent) of Americans think that the shark will win.

- While the vast majority (88 percent) of Americans know what event is taking place on August 18 in Las Vegas, just 34 percent know what country we're currently at war with.

- Nearly two thirds of all Dutch two-year-olds can recognize a picture of a bear and a shark.

- Almost 70 percent of Americans agree that the bear is more "fun and likable" than the shark.

- HardCorp has an overall approval rating of 71 percent, up from an all-time low of 18 percent two years ago.

- Sixty percent of Americans have bought at least one box of Sea-n-Lea Meat Snacks during the last six months.

- Almost half (46 percent) of Americans think that a shark is a mammal.

- Thirty-eight percent of Americans included the bear and/or the shark in their list of Five Most Important People of the Decade.

- Half of all Americans plan to watch the fight on PayView.

- Two percent of Americans have been to a cockfight.

- Of the 45 percent of Americans who believe in evolution, 58 percent believe that humans are direct descendants of bears.

- Asked what they would do if they ran into a bear or a shark, 36 percent of Americans said they would kill it, 33 percent said they would capture it, 22 percent said they would feed it, 8 percent said they would leave it alone or run away, and 1 percent said they would try to have sex with it.

- Sixty-eight percent of Americans do not know that both bears and sharks are on the Endangered Species list.

- Fourteen percent of Americans agree that good posture is pretty much the key to healthy living.

43

An Essay That Did Not Win

BEAR V. SHARK:
THE CLASSIC GAME OF STRATEGY
AND ENTERTAINMENT

(by C. H. Bachelder)

For 280 million or more players

Ages 0 to adult

Equipment: Major media, Internet, domed stadium, corporate sponsorship, First Amendment, patriotism, military bases, unemployment, sweatshops, complacent and politically impotent populace, homicide, crack cocaine, fashion, standardized tests

Setup: Give each player a Television, a second mortgage, a mind-numbing job, a staggering Visa debt, and a set of fast food action figures

Gameplay: Each player watches Television

Object: To perform meaningful work and forge rewarding connections with other human beings

Winning: Ha!

44

A Palpable Feeling

Are there personalized license plates on the Vegas-bound interstate? License plates with cryptic and clever little declarations of fealty? Man, like you wouldn't believe. There is a shorthand that you pick up after a while. For instance, BR = Bear. SHRK = Shark. LUV = Love. SUX = Sucks. You get the idea.

Mr. Norman says, "Maybe I should call the office."

Mrs. Norman, who at one time had touched Mr. Norman in extraordinary ways, in extraordinary places, who at one time had taken Mr. Norman's hand and guided him to places on her body, the existence of which he had previously heard about, sure, but never until those precise moments of contact quite believed in and which he now doubted once again because of the fallibility of memory, the corrosive work of the years, to tell the truth it might have been not Mrs. Norman at all but another woman, a previous girlfriend, a secretary at his place of employment, if it indeed happened at all, might have been a Television program, says, "Why?"

Mr. Norman says, "What?"

Mrs. Norman says, "Why should you call the office?"

Mr. Norman says, "I said I would."

Mrs. Norman says, "Then by all means."

Mr. Norman calls the office.

In the backseat Matthew says, "I've said it before: A shark is a killing machine."

In the backseat Curtis says, "Listen, have you *ever* seen a bear when the water is roily with salmon?"

A man at the office says, "Hello."

Mr. Norman says, "This is Larry Norman."

The man says, "Hey, Larry."

Mr. Norman says, "I'm just checking in."

The man says, "OK, thanks."

Mr. Norman says, "OK."

In the backseat Matthew says, "The shark is perfectly adapted to killing. Essentially it has not evolved in millions of years. God rendered it artfully."

In the front passenger seat Mrs. Norman says, "What do you mean by essentially?"

In the foreword, Aldous Huxley says, "Today it seems quite possible that the horror may be upon us in a single century."

Mr. Norman says, "How is everything?"

The man says, "Some high school principal in Wichita just ordered thirty fake laptops for his computer lab."

Mr. Norman says, "The kids will like those."

The man says, "Why don't you give us another call tomorrow, about the same time."

Mr. Norman says, "Will do."

The man says, "Listen, Larry, before you go. What kind of feeling are you getting out there in America?"

Mr. Norman says, "I don't know, a pretty good feeling."

The man says, "Yeah? Is the feeling palpable?"

Mr. Norman says, "Palpable?"

The man says, "Yeah, can you feel it?"

Mr. Norman says, "Can I feel the feeling?"

The man says, "Yeah, can you cut the feeling with a knife?"

Mr. Norman says, "I guess the feeling is fairly palpable."

The man says, "I just bet it is."

In the backseat the Television Personality says, "The latest polls show that of the 39 percent of Americans who know who Martin Van Buren is, 72 percent think that he was either 'better' or 'far better' than William Howard Taft."

In the backseat Curtis says, "Tafty Taft needs some PR."

In the office the man says, "Good-bye, Larry."

In the backseat Matthew says, *"Roily?"*

In the driver's seat Mr. Norman knows: A quick jerk of the wheel and it's all over.

45

Brevity is . . . wit

Now at the EPIcenter, when you purchase one epigraph (medium or large), we'll give you another epigraph (small, English language) absolutely free (offer not valid in all locations, check participating stores for details).

The EPIcenter provides the epitome of fast, reliable service. In addition to epigraphs, we also offer epigrams, epitaphs, epilogues, epithets, epistles, and other special orders for your Epicurean tastes.

We know you live in a hectic, fast-paced reading environment. We know that leisure time has gone the way of the leisure suit and the blue whale. We know it's true what they say: Brevity is . . . wit.

So let our trained epi-staff help you today. At the EPIcenter, we get to the point.

46

From Scene to Shining Scene

The American family just keeps driving the American vehicle across the American interstate system. Destination: the Sovereign Nation of Las Vegas.

There are specious skies, fruitless pains.

There is shredded grace.

There are amber waves of nausea.

There are purple billboards' majesty, countless billboards, just imagine how the earliest settlers must have felt gazing up at such wonders. These billboards—each one large enough to contain, say, cigarettes and beach volleyball, and sexy enough to prove a correlation between the two. A *strong* correlation. These billboards perform countless miracles of conjunction: cologne and power are joined in natural and sensible union, the corner office shown to be the telos of the fresh, manly scent; *bottled water* leads inexorably, syllogistically, to quirky individualism; baked cheese snacks and Happiness become indistinguishable; Seasoning Pouches and harmonious families reprise the chicken-or-the-egg conundrum.

A slightly sun-bleached Breakfast Link, hysterically enlarged to show texture and foregrounded against family members who clearly adore one another and who would want to get together *even if they weren't related,* says, "And I'm 80% meat!"

A casino promises fun for the whole family.

A politician promises fun for the whole family.

Gracious Native Americans selling authentic jewelry roadside at Gypsy strip malls promise to accept your check card, exit now.

An enormous digital clock—showing days, hours, minutes, seconds, split seconds—races countdown style toward Bear v. Shark II.

Curtis says, "I gotta pee like a *resource.*"

47

Mini-Death

The Normans pass Exit after Exit, Food Mart after Food Mart. Mr. Norman always has the uneasy feeling that he is passing up the best Food Mart and that he will inevitably stop at one that has disappointingly few variations on the corn chip, the individually wrapped cream-filled cake, the sweet carbonated beverage. It is difficult to tell the good Food Marts from the bad ones. The dashboard is oddly reticent. And the signs are of no help. Judging by the signs—on which "Quick" invariably becomes "Kwik" and *and* becomes *n*—you are led to believe that each store has the same commitment to expediency and convenience and variety, which is clearly not the case.

Are the Food Marts getting better, *funner,* as Las Vegas gets closer? It's an interesting premise, but I'm not sure it's true.

Food Mart, Food Mart, Food Mart. At the current rate, there will be more Food Marts than people in just twenty years. A nation of snacks and gas. It's the end of geography, the end of the road novel. Just try advancing a plot along the U.S. roadways. The Normans have traveled a distance of 302 miles (486 km), you'll have to take my word for it.

The Sport Utility Vehicle needs fuel and Matthew or Curtis—one of them back there—needs to pee, but it is difficult to choose a Food Mart. You feel that when you choose one, you rule out all the others. It is a loss, a mini-death. Robert Frost, a poet from New England, talks about that in one of his more well-known poems.

Mr. Norman pulls into a Gas-n-Dash, Pump 16. While Mrs. Norman and the boys go to the rest room, Mr. Norman puts fuel in the Sport Utility Vehicle and also washes the windshield.

A guy from Pump 22 says to Mr. Norman, "Say, where are you headed?"

Mr. Norman says, "What?"

The guy says, "Where are you headed?"

Mr. Norman says, "Las Vegas."

A sign with a little girl's picture on it says, "Have you seen me?"

The guy says, "Goin' to the big show?"

Mr. Norman says, "What?"

The guy says, "You going to see Bear versus Shark?" He actually says that, Bear *versus* Shark. Nobody says that. In today's hectic world, Mr. Norman thinks, who has time to say "versus"? It's always *vee*. Mr. Norman thinks maybe this guy is a foreigner, but he is speaking American.

Mr. Norman, vaguely suspicious, says, "Yes."

The Pump 22 guy says, "You must be excited."

Mr. Norman says, "I guess so."

The guy says, "Most people headed that way are pretty darn excited."

Mr. Norman says, "I'm pretty darn excited. It's palpable."

There are pretty puddles of gas. Rainbow puddles. A handwritten sign says, "Please prepay after dark."

The guy says, "I saw on the Television that they had a prefight workout yesterday and the bear looked great. Slim, alert, strong. Fur had sheen."

Mr. Norman says, "Sheen?"

The guy says, "Radiance. Luster."

Mr. Norman says, "Oh."

At a nearby plant where workers manufacture chips and circuit boards, a supervisor says, "We're going to have to let six hundred of you go."

The guy from Pump 22 crosses over the pump island and gets up close to Mr. Norman. His eyes are bright, clear, focused. There is obviously something wrong with him. He says, quietly, "Listen, there are other ways to live."

Mr. Norman says, "What?"

The creepy guy says, "I used to be like you. Worked in an office.

Babbled all the time, couldn't stop. Had the ESP TV, the downloaded uplinks, the personalized plates, the wife whose name occasionally escaped me, the whole five yards. But."

Mr. Norman says, "*Nine* yards."

The guy says, "What?"

Mr. Norman says, "The whole *nine* yards. You said five yards."

The Pump 22 guy says, "The exact yardage is not germane."

Mr. Norman says, "It's not like five yards would be *whole*."

The guy says, "All I'm saying."

Mr. Norman says, "Where do you suppose that saying came from? Football?"

The guy says, "Nine yards, whatever. The point is."

Mr. Norman says, "Fabric?"

The guy says, "There are other ways to live your life, better ways, take it from me. You find other people like us, you get rid of your Television."

Mr. Norman says, "Are you trying to sell me something? I already have a good Television. Several."

Mrs. Norman and the kids, bearing pretty decent Snacks, cross the parking lot toward the Sport Utility Vehicle.

Mr. Norman says, "I have to go now."

The guy says, "Just think about what I said."

Ariel Dorfman says, "We also have shields which can be used as mirrors."

The guy says, "We don't have much, but we're awake."

Mr. Norman gets into the Sport Utility Vehicle with his wife and their two children, Matthew and the other one, the younger one.

A sign says, "Persons with physical disabilities wishing to buy lottery tickets please sound horn for service."

Mrs. Norman says, "That man from Pump 22 had the kind of posture you read about."

Mr. Norman says, "His eyes were weird."

48

Like a Racehorse

Why, tell me this, would a racehorse have to pee so bad?

How do racehorses pee, anyway?

I mean, why would a racehorse have to pee more than, say, your average farm horse or your cantering beer-commercial horse?

Standing up?

And listen, is the idea here that they're sprinting *because* they have to pee, or is it the very act of sprinting that *causes* the need to urinate?

I don't believe they squat.

I can see it both ways.

They definitely don't lift a leg. I think they just let it rip.

Well, it depends on which type of horse you're talking about.

But we already specified that we're talking about racehorses.

You've got your stallions, your mares, your colts, your studs, your striplings—all pee different.

Palomino?

Different.

Pommel?

That one's sterile.

Yes, and so's the Earl Grey.

The thing you have to keep in mind is the withers.

Fetlock, croup, gaskin, hock.

Shank, pastern, muzzle.

Introduced by the Spaniards.

Hooves instead of feet.

You just better hold on tight bareback because I got this friend Billy who got thrown off one time and he busted up his gaskin pretty bad.

49

Princess Adelaide's Health

OK, joining us now is . . . Say, Mitch, ever get the sense that we're *forever* getting joined by people?

Oh yeah. Join join join. We're like a damn YMCA.

Did people ever say *joining us now* before, say, 1950?

Ridiculous.

So-and-so is joining us, so-and-so has joined us many times before, last summer we were joined by so-and-so.

That's what we do. We join. People join us.

Join now and save! Join now and receive a free tote bag!

Would you care to join us for dinner?

Let's join hands. Let's join forces.

We're like a movement or a cause or an Internet porn site.

Join starts to sound funny after a while, kind of like fork.

Join. Join. Join.

Fork. Fork.

Join.

OK, joining us today by satellite from London is . . . Hey, Mitch—

I know. You don't have to say it.

Back in the olden times, joining meant sharing the same physical space. If somebody joined you, then they were, like, *with* you.

Barbara, joining is no longer limited by considerations of space or time. Hell, on this very show we've been joined by former president Martin Van Buren as he orbited the moon in a lunar shuttle.

I know.

Join has undergone a revolution. Join has kept up. You have to keep up. If you don't, you get left in the dust. Join has reinvented itself. You have to hand it to join. Think of other verbs that have been left in the scrap heap of history, of interest only to crusty old professors.

I can't think of a single one.

That's my point.

There is a technology of joining, Mitch, a whole technology. The satellite uplinks, the remote feeds, underground cables in networks and webs. We're all joined. We want to keep in touch, but.

But perchance the first news that will leak through into the broad, flapping American ear will be that the Princess Adelaide has the whooping cough.

Hey, you've been reading Thoreau.

As you know, Barbara, he'll be joining us next week.

50

Accordion Knot

Back at cruising speed, it's family time: Mr. Norman calls home to retrieve phone messages while Mrs. Norman does a little back-to-school shopping for the boys on the Internet while Matthew plays Bear Killer and the other boy (the younger one) listens to headphones and plays Deep Sea Gore III and does some e-shopping for his main squeeze back home.

Matthew says, "Hey what's a Guardian knot?"

Mrs. Norman says, "I think you mean a Gordon knot."

Curtis, talking too loud because of his headphones, says, "I always thought it was Accordion knot."

Bear Killer says, "I vanquish thee."

Matthew says, "That doesn't make any sense."

Curtis says, "Well neither does Guardian knot, butt lick."

Mrs. Norman says, "Curtis, don't call Gordon a butt lick."

Matthew says, "It's Matthew."

Mrs. Norman says, "Each of your errors makes quite a bit of sense, each in their own special way."

Deep Sea Gore III says, "My femur is shattered, Hank."

Curtis says, "The Accordion knot was essentially a knot to tie up Phrygian bears, but the bears cut the knots with their pipin' swords."

The first day's drive is nearly complete.

Matthew says, "So how does Accordion knot, which is wrong, make sense and not Guardian knot?"

She (the answering machine) says, "You have fourteen new messages." Her voice is husky but demure. Wow.

Mr. Norman feels exhausted, but also something else.

Curtis, loudly, says, "In Cub Scouts we learned the carrick bend, the Blackwall hitch, and the slipknot."

Nauseated, yes, and dizzy. Bloated on sodium, goes without saying. Disoriented, numb.

Mrs. Norman says, "You won't get to tie up bears until Boy Scouts."

She (the answering machine) says, "Press one to review first message." So selfless, staying home to take messages while the family goes abroad.

But something else, too. There's something else in him besides the beat and burn of his heart.

Matthew says, "You could hold a bear with a damn granny knot."

The answering machine says, "Touch two to save message." That voice is something else. It's difficult to tell how sexually experienced she is.

He (Mr. Norman) feels restless, maybe that's it. No, not restless, exactly.

Curtis says, "Yeah, that's what the Phrygians thought, and then they got a little taste of bear steel."

She says, "Ooh, touch two *again*."

Lonesome.

51

Discussion Questions

1. An obscure and alarmist media critic once wrote, "In America we are never denied the opportunity to amuse ourselves." Write about a time when you were denied this fundamental right. How did it make you feel?

2. Explain the significance of the **archetype** of the journey in the **Western Literary Canon (WLC)**. Is the author employing and/or manipulating this archetype in this work? How does that make you *feel*?

3. Interview your family members and do some research on the Internet. Why or why not? Explain. Discuss. Compare and Contrast. Use appropriate Margins. Don't cheat. Don't disappoint us. Take the Princeton Review course whatever you do. Remember: The French and the Indians fought *together* during the French and Indian War, and how does that make you feel?

4. What does the use of present tense indicate about the utter obliteration of memory, history, and critical reflection, and what direction do you think hemlines will be moving in the fall?

5. Who do you think would win in a fight between a bear and a shark? Show your work.

6. Write about a time when Cultural Transmissions made you feel weak, passive, obedient, vertiginous, alienated, isolated, atomized, brand-loyal, spiritually comatose, compliant, simultaneously gullible and cynical, politically impotent, numb. *How did this make you feel?*

7. Italo Calvino once wrote, "Satire is not the approach [to comedy] that I find most congenial. One component of satire is moralism, and another is mockery. Anyone who plays the moralist thinks he is better than others, whereas anyone who goes in for mockery thinks he is smarter. In any case, satire excludes an attitude of questioning and of questing." Well, then. Gosh. (a) Do you find this book to be roiling with moralism and mockery? (b) Do you think the author thinks he is better and smarter than you? (c) How does this make you feel? (d) How do you think this makes the author feel, lying in bed in the dark? (e) Don't you think the author lying in the dark often wishes he had written a more serious and *questing* book? (f) With penetrating insights into the human heart? (g) Don't you just kind of get the sense that the author masks his sorrows behind layers of jokes, this chapter being one of them? (h) The word *roiling* being one of them? (i) Each damn character being one of them? (j) Didn't Barthelme do this quiz stunt back in like 1965 or something? (k) Would you believe that the author is genuinely sorry? (l) Beneath the crusty strata of irony? (m) Sad and sorry? (n) And do you think that maybe, with all due respect to Mr. Calvino, yet another element of satire is the satirist's heartfelt and heartbroken sense that things really could be better than they are? (o) Much better? (p) Why point it out and make fun of it otherwise? (q) Aren't satirists just sentimental and oversensitive cranks who just wish the world were a kinder place and furthermore sort of believe that it could be a kinder place and it is therefore tragic that it's such a cruel and stupid place? (r) Do you think you might like to come over to the author's little apartment sometime to talk and have coffee if he promised not to be so arch and droll? (s) Not even for that long, maybe like forty-five minutes? (t) If he apologized for the whole bear porn thing? (u) Doesn't it seem like that could be neat and meaningful? Please discuss.

52

www.bearnaked.com

Click here for the world's raunchiest ursine porn site. We've got hundreds of hot, wet bear sluts, just the way you like 'em!

We've got bear onion, bear beaver, bears in panties, bears in leather, bear on bear, two girls and a bear, teen bear, circus bear whores who can't get enough, Big Mama bears with eight titties, schoolgirl bears, French maid bears who love to go down, bears in bondage, dildo bears, cubs, doggy-style bears, bears in heat, footlong bears, sleeping bears, and much, much more.

Visa and MasterCard accepted. Must be 12 or over.

53

Plugged Inn

The Normans locate their hotel off of the interstate. It's a Plugged Inn, a quaint new American-style chain that offers, in its upscale rooms, two Televisions, Internet access, and scores of virtual amenities, as well as a real swimming pool.

The idea is that you can *stay connected in style*. It's like you can work and play just like you were at home, except you're not at home, you're in a hotel room somewhere. The idea is that you never—I mean *never*—have to miss a cop show or a video conference or a sexy chat-room discussion. It just doesn't matter how far you are from home. It's really *just like* being at home, except much smaller and more expensive.

Mr. Norman, heck, what a long drive, says, "What?"

Mrs. Norman reboots.

While Curtis programs his General Topics of Personal Interest, Matthew programs his General Topics of Personal Interest.

Mr. Norman says, "How about a swim?"

Mr. Norman's family stares at Mr. Norman, six eyes on the guy who said *swim*. Mrs. Norman actually does a double take, sitcom style. *Nails it.* Then, realizing what she's done, she does it again—a second double take, that's four takes in all—but this second double take is stilted, mechanical, self-conscious, and she knows it.

She (Mrs. Norman) says, "Shoot."

Curtis's GTPI: Martial Arts, Extreme Stocks & Bonds, Australian Rules Football, Art with Blood, Window Treatments, the Dutch.

Mr. Norman says, "Come on, honey, let's take a dip." He looks at her, well, funny. He winks and twitches. He says, "There's nobody in the pool right now."

Mrs. Norman says, "What?"

Mr. Norman says, "No lifeguard on duty."

Mrs. Norman says, "But I want to check the Internet to see where we've gone today." She logs on at the bedside port.

Matthew watches a show that shows a blindfolded contestant touching a series of objects and guessing which one is her husband.

Outside the real window the sun sets in pretty chemical hues.

Curtis's picture: Edgy handheld footage of inexpensive home-made curtains.

Picture in picture: Edgy faux low-budget handheld footage of a dike.

A woman on Matthew's Television says, "Now *this* is Paul, I just know it."

Mr. Norman mutilates his swimming trunks with a pair of scissors built into his watch.

Dent Trilling, the Game Show Host on Matthew's Television, says, "Oooh, sorry, Mrs. Tanner, that's not your spouse. Would you believe it's a *chinchilla*?"

Mrs. Norman stares into the bedside monitor, reviewing the day's journey, nodding. She says, "No wonder it was so fun."

Mr. Norman studies his twitching and winking in the mirror. He says softly to his wife, "I'm going down to the pool. I'll see you in a few minutes, you hot thing."

Mrs. Norman's double take lacks that certain something.

Curtis's Television says, "The blue chips are pipin'."

Matthew's Television says, "See you next week on . . . [audience yells along] . . . *THAT'S . . . NOT . . . YOUR . . . SPOUSE!*"

Offstage Paul Tanner says to crying wife, "Mind telling me how the *fuck* you mistake me for a small South American rodent raised for its silvery gray fur?"

54

Non Sequitur

A Television Personality says, OK, we just have about thirty seconds left. Tell us about your new self-published book.

The new self-published book author says, My main point, Carol, is that our culture's information practices have just about done away with the concept of a non sequitur. In other words, we now fully expect things not to follow from other things, such that when things do not follow from other things, they seem to follow quite naturally from other things.

The Television Personality says, Well, you lost me, I'm afraid.

The new self-published book author says, The real non sequitur has perhaps become the sequitur, so to speak.

The Television Personality says, Whoa, the sequitur, huh?

The Television Show Director says, Five seconds.

The Television Show Producer says, Remind me never to have another author on the show.

Roland Barthes (author of *Mythologies*) says, In fact, nothing can be safe from myth.

The new self-published book author says, When a point follows another point it seems not to follow at all because we expect it not to follow and when it doesn't it seems as if it does because we expected it not to.

That's a wrap.

The Television Commercial says, If you have lung cancer, would you rather go to some general practitioner or to a lung cancer specialist? At Green Paint, we don't just dabble in greens like other paint companies. Green is what we do. So whether you need a lime or a forest, a pea or a hunter, a sage or a kelly, come to Green Paint, where green has been a specialty for over twenty years. And remember: We do lawns.

55

Patented Flap

In the dark, heavily chlorinated pool of the Plugged Inn, Mr. Norman twitches and rubs himself against the shivering Mrs. Norman.

Through chattering teeth Mrs. Norman says, "Fresh minty taste."

Things are going pretty well.

The poolside Television says, "Nobody wants to be constipated as a result of their diarrhea medicine."

Mr. Norman takes Mrs. Norman's hand and places it on his, well, penis, which is protruding into the chlorine through a hole he has cut in the crotch of his swimming trunks. In the water, his erection looks bent and wavy. It appears to squiggle and pulse. Desire refracted.

Mrs. Norman gasps.

Mr. Norman twitches sexily. He winks at her with an eye all red from driving and pool chemicals. His wet hair sticks up funny.

Mrs. Norman says, "Larry."

Mr. Norman says, "I saw it on the Television."

Mrs. Norman says, "I saw it, too. Interesting program on prison sex."

Mr. Norman says, "Prisoners are still people."

He kisses Mrs. Norman on the neck. He licks her, tastes the urine and chlorine. Who would win in a fight between Dirty and Clean?

A dead cricket floats past.

Mrs. Norman says, "Larry, I bought those swimming trunks at Griffith's. They're durable, yet sporty. They're safe to one hundred meters. They dry quickly and they've got a special patented Antichafe Flap."

Mr. Norman gazes down into the dark water at his patented trunks, his shimmering flagellum.

Mrs. Norman says, "You cut the flap, Larry."

Mr. Norman says, "We'll just get another pair." He gropes Mrs. Norman underwater.

A sign outside the pool says, "The management requests that you relax, enjoy your stay with us, and don't pee in the pool."

Mrs. Norman says, "We can't get another pair. I got them at a going-out-of-business sale. Sixty percent off."

Mr. Norman stops groping and twitching. He pushes the wavy thingy back into his trunks. It pops out again.

He says, "Sixty percent off everything or just specially marked items?"

A third-floor balcony Television says, "Plenty of head rheum."

The Normans bob and tread, locked and awkward.

Mrs. Norman says, "Ouch."

Mr. Norman says, "This is not exactly what I want. It's sort of close, though."

Mrs. Norman says, "Not here."

Mr. Norman says, "I mean, don't you just worry about the children?"

Mrs. Norman says, "Every day of my life."

56

Shark's Belly

Ever see inside a shark's belly, like on Television?
Who hasn't?
Like when they split the shark open?
Stock footage.
All kinds of detritus and flotsam.
Damn junkyard.
Tires, oil drums—
Other sharks' bellies, human babies—
Trees, pirate ships—
Robots, anchors—
Plankton, scrod—
Scuba gear, driftwood—
Tacos, wildflowers—
Hash browns—
Gold ingots—
Wiener dogs.
Buoyed lagan, in general.
Not a fussy eater.
No.
Literally needs to eat or it will die.
Two stomachs like a cow.
Three's what I heard.

*　　*　　*

Hey you still awake?

Yeah.

Ever sat in the back of a pickup at a county dump in almost-Canada Minnesota and watched the running of the northern lights?

The oriole bolus.

And then when you're kind of drunk on PBR and about asleep and think you done missed what you came to see you wake up and see the thick silhouettes of bears amongst the rubbish and offal?

All in the dumpsters. Upside down and whatnot.

Ain't been built a refuse containment system can keep out a bear.

Among its attributes is a steely caginess and paws that work like hands.

And a love of syrup.

Not the lite kind, either.

Shit.

57

A Subtle Weapon of Mass Destruction

Mr. Norman can't sleep, what's new.

The Televisions cast entertaining shadows on the walls.

In the next bed over, Mr. Norman's sons talk steadily in their sleep, an ongoing conversation that comes together and then moves apart, loosely braided, like two plastic vines climbing an imitation oak.

Beside him, Mrs. Norman is asleep, snoring quietly, her headphones whispering encouragement to her vertebrae.

Mr. Norman gets dressed and wanders the halls of the Plugged Inn. He can hear his fellow travelers in their boxes. In one room, a couple is having a loud and passionate fight, but it turns out to be just the Television. In another room, a couple is fucking up a storm, but it turns out to be just the Television. In other rooms, a father teaches his little girl how to fish, a family mourns the death of a grandmother, a man talks to his favorite beer, a woman successfully juggles a career and all domestic responsibilities.

The non-Television people are quiet. It's like they're not even in there.

Mr. Norman walks the mazes of the Plugged Inn, looking for something, he knows not what. Something: A smooth, dry, cold-filtered, ice-brewed Brew with no Bitter Aftertaste? A twin-cam engine? A Hearty Snack that will tide him over? Perhaps an expensive and stylishly shoddy haircut that says to the world, Why should I care about my hair when there is so much else to worry about like ozone and poverty?

He (Mr. Norman), hair stylelessly shoddy, ends up at the small Television lounge on the third floor. The door is closed. He hears voices inside.

One voice (the Television?) says, "All the lard with none of the guilt."

Another voice (Plotter No. 1) says, "Look, I hate Asians as much as anyone, but we can't blow up the whole fucking country of Las Vegas."

Another voice (Plotter No. 2) says, "Well we damn sure got to blow up *something*."

The closed door is unlocked and Mr. Norman opens it. He would like some company.

In the center of the room is a group of about seven or eight burly men with wild, round eyes, gathered loosely around a large map and a case of Hernia Soda. The men all stare at Mr. Norman. Some of them point guns at him.

One of the burly, wild-eyed men says, "What's the password?"

Mr. Norman, on a family trip to see Bear v. Shark II, having a little difficulty sleeping, out wandering the halls, just looking for something to want, says, "What?"

The men put down their guns. One of them says, "Get in here already. Grab yourself a Herney."

Another one says, "I thought we might see you here tonight."

Mr. Norman pulls up a chair and joins the loose circle of men. It feels good to be a part of something.

One of the burly fellows says, "Listen, we all agree, do we not, that Bear v. Shark is a disease, a cancer, a subtle weapon of mass destruction unleashed on this nation by crafty, hardworking dog-eaters who seek world dominance."

Another stocky plotter says, "Well put."

The articulate burly guy continues. He says, "And further, we all agree that the best way to strike a blow against our skinny yellow foes is to detonate something."

The men say, "Here here."

Mr. Norman feels that something is not quite right, and yet the logic of it all has him in a stranglehold.

The Television says, "Are you sick and tired of your ugly shins?"

Mr. Norman is getting sleepy. He says, "The look and feel of real pork."

The well-spoken schemer says, "And since we can't really blow up all of Vegas, that leaves us with either a casino, an elementary school, or an assisted-living community. I say we vote. Let's see a show of hands for the casino."

A Plugged Inn security guard comes through the door and tips his cap to the hate group.

Mr. Norman yawns and offers the guard a Hernia Soda.

58

Textual Evidence

OK, we're back. Before we continue our conversation with Dr. Underwood.

I'm not really a doctor.

I want to remind listeners to check out our Web site at double-u double-u double-u dot bloodbathmania all one word dot com forward slash democratic spirit forward slash public pulse forward slash freedom. Once you're there, you can vote, you can purchase merchandise, you can see who your favorite celebrities are pulling for, you can read Facts for Fence-Sitters, and you can take a quiz to see how closely you match the general profile of a bear or a shark fan. Also, you can e-mail us with your answer to our Question of the Week. As you know, last Saturday a Cincinnati man won a radio station's ticket giveaway promotion by eating his own hand up to the wrist.

Whoa.

And so this week we want to know: "What would *you* do for a ticket to Bear v. Shark II?"

Be creative, folks.

Now then, Dr. Underwood.

I'm ABD, actually.

It is your contention that Shakespeare had bear sympathies.

Yes.

On what basis would you make this claim?

Well, textual evidence. An on-line Shakespeare concordance shows well over four hundred references to *bear* or *bears* in the plays.

And fewer references to sharks?

Just two. In *Hamlet,* we've got young Fortinbras *sharking* up lawless resolutes in Norway's skirts, and then.

Then of course the witches in Macbeth.

Yes, of course.

They throw the maw and gulf of the ravined salt-sea shark into that brew. Right, Doc?

Yes.

Toil and *trouble.* That's pretty fearsome stuff. Did they put any ravined bear parts in there?

The shark is minor in Shakespeare. You'll find far more goats, crabs, whales, newts, worms, wolves, dolphins, sheep, and of course bears.

So how would you respond, Dr. Underwood, to Newman's elegant "negative evidence thesis"—that is, the alarming paucity of sharks in Shakespeare is indicative of the Bard's terror of, and respect for, these marine killers?

I think that's silly. There's also an alarming paucity of station wagons in Shakespeare, but you don't see me trying to build a career on it.

The maw and gulf of the ravined salt-sea shark. *Wow.* Sorry, that is just terrifying stuff, Doc.

Listen, in *Romeo and Juliet* we've got roaring bears, in *The Tempest* we've got angry bears, in *Troilus and Cressida* we've got churlish bears, and in *Lear* we've got head-lugged bears. In *The Winter's Tale,* we've got a guy exiting, pursued by a bear.

Head-lugged?

Dragged by a chain around the head, and thus surly.

What does *ravined* mean?

And in *Macbeth,* V.vii, we've got Big Mac saying, I cannot fly, But bear-like I must fight the course.

Scene *seven*?

Yes.

Doesn't Macbeth *die* while fighting bear-like?

That's not the point.

How would you respond to the claim that Shakespeare was writing some four hundred years before Bear v. Shark was formulated?

I'd call that the worst kind of historical provincialism. Bear v. Shark is just the most recent cultural articulation of an archetypal binary.

And how would you respond to the claim that the overwhelming majority of bear references in Shakespeare are verbs and not animals?

You know sometimes it's like Freud never happened.

I'm thinking *As You Like It*, II.iv, Celia says, I pray you bear with me; I cannot go further, and Touchstone says, For my part, I had rather bear with you than bear you; yet I should bear no cross if I did bear you; for I think you have no money in your purse. Sure, a lot of bears here, Doc, but they're not talking about grizzlies.

It's like, post-Freud, I can't believe two people could be having this conversation. Verb *bears,* far more so than noun *bears,* are proof of the Bard's deep obsession.

You're saying expression of the unconscious.

Yes.

And how much credence do you give to the fact that an anagram of Shakespeare is *A shark's epee*?

I give it precisely as much credence as it deserves. It's not scholarship.

Dr. Underwood, how have your ideas been accepted in the academic community?

They have been accepted as all dangerous truths hath e'er been accepted.

Well good for you. We wish you continued success.

59

The Shark's Neck

Mr. Norman wakes up in the small Television lounge of the Plugged Inn. The hate group is gone. Was there really a hate group in the lounge or was there just a realistic Television program about a hate group? Mr. Norman wonders what happened to the group. Cops probably got those guys, unless it's a two-parter. Tune in next week.

A small scrap of paper underneath Mr. Norman's stuffed chair says, "We'll see you in Vegas."

Mr. Norman looks at his watch for the time, but it's all temperature, altitude, important phone numbers. What the hell time is it?

He (Mr. Norman) says, "It's a cold bowl of chili when love lets you down."

The Television says, "Do you want to roll or pass, Darrell?"

Toby Wiley, eleven, of Statesville, N.C., says, "I'd drink real piss for a ticket."

Shit, what time is it? Mr. Norman's watch is all color, logo, design. It's gorgeous, this thing.

Mr. Norman walks back to his room, where his family is watching Television and packing their bags.

Mrs. Norman says, "I was just looking for you. Did you get my e-mail?"

Mr. Norman says, "I'm tired of my ugly shins."

The Normans walk to the lobby for checkout and complimentary Continental Breakfast.

Mr. Norman says, "Calvin, what do you know about the Round-Eyed Sons of the Knightly Order?"

Curtis says, "It's Curtis."

Mr. Norman says, "Don't get fresh, Cal."

Curtis says, "They're a hate group, Dad. Nutbags. They've been blowing stuff up, hanging bears and sharks in refugee. The sharks never stay strung up on account of no necks."

Mr. Norman says, "It's *apogee,* son."

Matthew says, "Technically, the shark does have a neck."

Mrs. Norman says, "Why would anyone be opposed to bears and sharks? They're beautiful creatures, each one in their own way."

An unsupervised drowning kid in the pool says, "Help."

Mr. Norman says, "Come to think of it, they did seem a little suspicious."

Curtis says, "Steer clear of RESKO, Dad."

In line for juice substitute, a burly traveling software salesman with a philosophy degree and an extensive criminal record says, "I would have preferred the *analytic* breakfast."

The guy looks familiar to Mr. Norman.

Curtis says to the traveling software salesman, "Do you have a Web site?"

Tiny diamonds of white morning sun shimmer on the wet, flailing arms of the unsupervised drowning kid.

Curtis and the felon swap business cards and promise to keep in touch.

60

Bear v. Shark:
The Quiz

Test your knowledge of bears and sharks with this fun True or False quiz. The answers can be found in Chapter 82.

1. Sharks do not have tongues.

2. The polar bear and the Kodiak (North American brown) bear are the largest members of the bear family.

3. Sharks have poor vision.

4. Almost all bears are omnivorous. The koala bear is the only herbivorous bear.

5. Blue sharks, the most prolific of the shark family, generally give birth to 25–50 pups at one time, and occasionally a "litter" will consist of 100 pups or more.

6. Bears preparing for hibernation will eat up to 20,000 calories per day.

7. The whale shark, which occasionally reaches a length of 50 feet or more, is the largest fish.

8. Bears actually appear in the fossil record prior to sharks.

9. Some sharks can predict the future.

10. Bear gallbladders, believed to have medicinal properties, fetch a high price on the black markets of Eastern countries.

11. Shark attacks cause an average of 25 human fatalities each year.

12. During hibernation—a period of 2–7 months—bears do not need to eat, drink, urinate, or defecate.

61

Seven-Second Delay

In the backseat Curtis is talking on a cell phone. He says, "Hi."

Then he says, "Oh, pretty good."

Mrs. Norman says, "Mind if we turn on the radio?"

Mr. Norman says, "You know, I hardly remember anything about my childhood."

A Talk Radio Host says, "OK, time to take some calls. This is Omar from Fairbanks, Alaska. Hi, Omar."

Omar says, "Hi."

Curtis says, "I have two questions, really."

Mr. Norman says, "I see pictures from when I was a kid and it's like it's someone else."

The Talk Radio Host says, "How's life treating you up there in Fairbanks?"

Curtis says, "First, what is your stance on the whole shark-on-ark debate? I mean, it just seems like Noah would have needed some kind of holding tank, which was probably not feasible for early sailing vessels."

Omar says, "Oh, pretty good."

Mrs. Norman says, "Don't you think that's how it is for everyone?"

The Talk Radio Host says, "Omar, what's your question for Reverend Hollis?"

Mr. Norman says, "Maybe so."

Omar from Alaska says, "I have two questions, really."

The Talk Radio Host says, "OK, fire away, Omar."

Mrs. Norman says, "I mean, those people, us, that we see in pictures are younger, fresher, they have better shins. It's hard to identify with them."

Omar says, "First, what is your stance on the whole shark-on-ark debate? I mean, it just seems like Noah would have needed some kind of holding tank, which was really probably not feasible for early sailing vessels."

Mrs. Norman says, "Ooh, interesting question. Curt, are you listening to this?"

Curtis says, *"Yes, ma'am."*

Reverend Hollis says, "Well, as you know, that question is stirring up quite a bit of controversy right now. Many bear-leaning biblical scholars and Televangelists have argued, based on the so-called Holding Tank Thesis you mentioned, that there could not have been sharks on the ark, and thus the animal is probably a creature that the Devil sent to earth to destroy bears and other noble vertebrates, such as humans."

Omar says, *"Yes, ma'am."*

Mr. Norman says, "But the scary thing is that it's not just my childhood. I have trouble remembering anything about my life, even from a week ago."

Curtis says, "That is such horseshit, Reverend."

A radio censor says, "Kill that."

Mr. Norman says, "And then I think maybe it's best that I don't remember. Maybe the truly scary thing is that there's really nothing much to remember."

Reverend Hollis says, "However, Omar, there is some evidence to support the claims now being made that Noah or perhaps a pious cabin boy could have kept sharks alive by wrapping them in wet sacks or baggies, or even by just chaining them to the deck. After all, there was plenty of rain."

Curtis says, "Who do you think would win in a fight between a bear and one of the disciples?"

The Talk Radio Host says, "Yeah, a real *frog*-strangler, Reverend."

The Talk Radio Host says, "Omar, what's your second question for Reverend Hollis?"

Mrs. Norman says, "Larry, I think you're probably just tired from work and all this driving."

Omar says, "Who do you think would win in a fight between a bear and one of the disciples?"

Curtis says, "Oh, I don't know, Luke?"

Mr. Norman says, "Well, I am tired, but I think maybe there's something else, like there's some switch that never got switched."

Reverend Hollis says, "Well, that really depends on which one you're talking about. I wouldn't want to make some blanket statement. Did you have anyone in mind?"

Mrs. Norman says, "Switch?"

Omar says, "Oh, I don't know, Luke?"

Mr. Norman says, "Yeah, like a feeling switch or something."

Reverend Hollis says, "Oh, well there is some evidence to suggest that Luke was narcoleptic and really skinny, so I wouldn't want to plop a lot of money down on him. And same goes for Paul—Paul would be hopelessly outmatched, that goes without saying."

Mr. Norman says, "Curtis, Matthew?"

Mrs. Norman says, "Matthew's asleep, honey."

Reverend Hollis says, "Now Mark, Mark is a different story. Mark was scrappy and he had very good speed for his size, and so I'd want to say he'd have a decent shot against a bear, Omar."

Mr. Norman says, "Curtis, do you ever feel like, I don't know, like something's wrong or something's missing?"

Curtis says, "No."

Mrs. Norman says, "Larry, he's just a kid."

The Talk Radio Host says, "That's interesting, Reverend."

Mr. Norman says, "But that's when the switch switches. Or doesn't switch."

The Talk Radio Host says, "Omar, any more questions for Reverend Hollis?"

Omar says, "No."

Mr. Norman says, "Listen, Curt, if you ever feel like something's not right, even if you don't know quite what it is, I want you to come talk to me."

Curtis says, "I will."

Mr. Norman says, "That's good, buddy. I'm here for you."

Reverend Hollis says, "Thanks for the tough questions, Omar."

The Talk Radio Host says, "Yes, thanks, Omar, and give everyone in Fairbanks a big bear hug for us."

Omar says, "I will."

62

We Know You Know

Psssst. Hey, you. The smart one there, surrounded by those zombie robots all dolled up in the latest fashions and chattering on and on about bears and sharks. Yeah, you. Listen up.

Look, we here at Sexy Pants know that you know that a damn pair of pants, even a pair of Sexy Pants, is not going to make you happy, fulfilled, or even Sexy. And hey, we know that you know that we know it.

And we know, too, that you see all those vapid little consumers in the mall dropping their hard-earned cash for expensive pants that are just going to leave them feeling all empty in their souls and in their wallets.

But you, now you're different. You're cut from a different cloth, just like Sexy Pants. You're onto the game, and you're not going to let it play you.

So set yourself apart from the rest. Wear Sexy Pants.

Because Savvy is Sexy.

63

An Outreach Situation

OK, relax. Tell us what happened. Start at the beginning.

He just started beating the crap out of me. I don't have any arms in that shark costume and I couldn't defend myself.

Wait, wait. Back up. What were you doing at the elementary school?

San Francisco 3, Florida 2.

The fighting is not supposed to be real.

OK, relax.

Have you found Bobby yet?

We're looking for Bobby. Just settle down and tell the story from the start.

Atlanta 10, Philadelphia 2.

Well, me and Bobby travel around to different schools, you know. We wear these furry costumes. I'm the shark and he's the bear.

The shark costume is furry?

Well, yeah, the fur is not as shaggy as the bear fur. But it's hard to make a suit with the look and feel of real cartilage.

I understand.

My mother made the suits.

Her name?

New York Mets 3, Montreal 1.

Agnes.

So who do you work for?

I work for the highway department.

The highway department pays you to visit schools in bear and shark costumes?

What? No, no. We just do that for fun. Volunteer basis.

Giving back to the community.

An outreach situation.

Go ahead.

Milwaukee 6, Cincinnati 5.

So we travel around and talk to the kids. In our costumes.

Is it hot in there? In the costumes?

Oh God, you wouldn't believe it. And it stinks, too. But listen, you gotta be tough. If you pass out, those kids will start kicking you. I learned that the hard way.

You talk to the children.

Yes. They just seem to relate to us. I have a hard time talking to my own kids, you know, but when I put on that shark costume, it's like all of a sudden I have a way with the youngsters. They respond to me. They respect me.

Houston 8, St. Louis 1.

And what do you and Bobby speak to the kids about?

Well, just whatever. Excuse me a second. . . . Sorry. That guy beat the hell out of me. Have you found him?

We're working on it, sir.

My feet are together in the back fin, you know? I don't have very good balance. He just pushed me right over.

You were saying.

Well, we have a drugs and alcohol talk we give. One time, after a fourth grader accidentally shot Bobby in the snout, we gave a firearms safety talk. We talk about venereal disease, good sportsmanship, study habits. Sometimes we make it into a science and nature lesson, though that's not really my field.

Right.

Chicago 9, Pittsburgh 5.

We just sit up there, you know, no fancy lights or music. No prepared speeches or anything like that. Just a bear and a shark connecting with the children.

And then you fight?

Yeah, usually the kids ask for it and we'll end our session by wrestling a little bit. Just for fun, you know. Not serious fighting. Rolling around on the carpet, under the desks, growling and stuff. They love it. Bobby does this karate thing.

Los Angeles 4, San Diego 3.

And when did you sense that something was wrong today?

Well, about midway through our talk, I knew it wasn't Bobby in that bear suit. I could hear him breathing real heavy in there and his voice sounded strange and he was giving bad advice to the kids.

Such as?

He said he thought it was a good idea to take a few years off between elementary school and middle school. Hitchhike around, see the world.

And then.

And then I'm getting worried because where's Bobby? But I'm a performer. You have to go on with the show. Colorado 18, Arizona 13. And I think that it was actually a decent show because the bear and I were disagreeing a lot and the kids sort of got to witness a debate.

And then you fought.

Well, yeah, the kids asked for it. And I was a bit worried. And I whispered to this guy, Hey, go easy, but then he pushed me over and started beating and kicking me. The kids loved it. He cracked two ribs.

And then did he snatch the little girl?

He stood on my neck first.

And then he snatched the girl?

Yes. He grabbed a laptop computer in one paw and that little girl in the other. She was screaming and giggling, the kids were cheering. I threw up in my suit.

Anaheim 9, Seattle 7.

And then he left?

Yes, he took off. And you haven't found him?

We're working on it.

And Bobby?

We're working on it, sir.

And the girl?

We did find her, I'm afraid.

Christ.

What?

I can't get a goddamn Yankees score.

64

Cancer

At lunch, the Normans stop at a place called Surf-n-Surf, a seafood joint with unlimited Internet access and cable Television in every booth.

Mrs. Norman has crab cakes and a game show.

Matthew and Curtis have fish sticks and bear cabaret.

Mr. Norman goes to the bathroom. He doesn't feel all that well. He feels terrible. Not terrible, but not so great. Or maybe he feels OK, normal. How do you know how you feel? An X ray, a thermometer, a blood test. You need equipment. Otherwise how do you know how you feel? He thinks it's probably cancer. What is cancer, anyway? Everyone has it, everyone gets it, some people die and some people don't, but nobody really knows what it is. Sometimes it's malign, sometimes it's indignant. It's a fungus. It's in your cells. You can see cells in cork in high school biology class. The tumors grow in the wet dark of you. The cancerous cells spread through your system like news on the wire. Like *bad* news: A school shooting, an earthquake, an assassination, a baby in a well, a baby with seizures, a baby with no brain, a baby in the trash, mass starvation, prison camps, cats being used in cat food, mass layoffs, cancer, war, airplane crashes, drugs, disloyalty, cruelty, lies, rain that never stops, rain that never comes. Mr. Norman thinks cancer probably smells like fish, like fake fish microwaved in an interstate restaurant. Mr. Norman does not know what cancer is, what causes it, how you cure it. He doesn't know anything about his own body. His eyes point outward and his insides are a dark, damp mystery. Turns out his heart is not shaped like a heart at all and heartburn has to do with the eructation of acidic fluid toward the esophagus. It's a pump, the heart, and the brain is the command center. It sends messages. It tells things to do things. It's a computer. It's so easy to get game scores and stock prices, but where is my kidney and how do I feel? What is cancer and why do I have it or not have it?

Mr. Norman pees into a trough shaped like a tuna.

The graffiti says, "Bear cubs wanted."

The graffiti says, "The D Dome is gonna blow."

The graffiti says, "There's a cure in TeleTown."

The graffiti says, "Commies & Cookies."

The graffiti says, "The fish sticks are shark dicks."

In a stall, behind a closed door, a man cries out in pain.

The lights buzz and flicker. The piped-in radio says, "We're overstocked. Everything's got to go."

Mr. Norman opens his mouth and stares into the bathroom mirror. Are those taste buds or cancer bumps?

The man in the stall says, "Oh God, no."

65

Virtual Interview

The interviewer, in a comfortable chair facing an empty comfort-able chair in a warmly lit room, says earnestly to nobody, "Nina, why did you write *How to Talk to Your Children about Bear v. Shark*?"

Nina Bowen, in a comfortable chair in a warmly lit room that is months and miles away from the warmly lit room in which the inter-viewer posed his question, says to a stand-in, some technical assis-tant, "I just saw a need for it, Todd. There's been a knee-jerk reaction among some parents concerning the violence, and I understand this impulse but I think it is misguided."

Todd, the interviewer, says, "Explain." He probably does twenty takes of "Explain." Some of his "explains" are sympathetic, guiding, others are borderline hostile, others are curious with raised eyebrows. The editors take their pick.

Nina, the author, says, "Well, Todd, if we complain about the vio-lence of Bear v. Shark—if we make a fuss about it or even forbid our children to watch it or talk about it or research it on the Internet or read on-line comic books about it or play with their video games or electronic action figures—then I think we're sending a subtle but strong message that there is something wrong or unnatural or shame-ful in this violence. And I think that's a damaging message to send."

Todd says, "Explain."

Nina, also the author of *Rethinking Smut,* says to the technical assistant with bad skin, "Todd, the natural world is violent. Why should we censor this? Violence is very natural, just look around you. Bears and sharks fight for their lives every day. They don't generally fight each other, but they fight violent battles to stay alive. This violence is part of the natural order, and I think our children need to understand this and not be ashamed of it or afraid of it. We can't shield them."

Todd, the interviewer, says, "I see."

It's not a very strong "I see," he's certainly capable of better, but it's the best of his six takes.

66

Entertainment Exhaust

Tell about the American landscape.

Pavement, Cancer, Food Marts, Wires & Cables, Bumper Stickers, Billboards, Weather. Some of it's real pretty, still.

Tell about the border towns.

Once you get within about twenty-five miles of Vegas, the border towns start popping up. Last chance for cheap beer, last chance for cheap gas, that kind of thing.

Tell about TeleTown.

TeleTown is down in a very big canyon, you wouldn't say nestled. The interstate runs over the top of it. This town is large, sprawling.

Tell about how you get there.

There are Exits located conveniently at either end of the canyon.

Tell about the people who live there.

Looks to me like pretty poor and desperate folks.

Tell about what they do.

They watch Television.

Tell about how they make their living.

They make these special cookies and sell them to tourists. They're good, real gingery.

Tell about what else they do.

Don't know what else they do. Watch Television, by the looks of it.

Tell about how at night or even on an overcast day.

At night or even on an overcast day if you drive the long bridge over TeleTown you can see the flickering glow of a million Televisions. This glow, it hangs low over the town like a huge bank of blue-gray fog. It's entertainment exhaust and it's beautiful.

Tell about how it's not much of a town.

Just huts and hovels, tepees and lean-tos. A couple miles across. One big Gypsy camp lit up by the glow of a million Televisions. But not, you know, filthy. No shit in the streets, that kind of thing.

Tell about irony.

It's *tyrannical.*

Tell what else D. F. Wallace says about it.

It's bigger than ever after 30 long years as the dominant mode of hip expression. It's not a rhetorical mode that wears well.

Tell about the new rebels.

They won't be scared of sentimentality or melodrama.

Tell about the Normans.

They're passing over TeleTown. It's an overcast day. They can see the glow. They're going to exit because they've heard about the cookies.

Tell about how they treat Mr. Norman.

They know his name when he gets there. They ask him to stay awhile, have a look around. See how things work.

Tell about their eyes.

Strange look to them. Alert, clear. What's the opposite of glassy?

Tell about how nobody is fat in TeleTown.

Well, I doubt they have much food to eat.

But still.

Nobody is fat in TeleTown. Almost nobody.

Tell about how nobody seems to be watching all those Televisions.

It's true.

There is beautiful wooden furniture there, isn't there? And these incredible wicker baskets and quilts. What's that about?

Your guess is as good as mine.

The cats all look peaceful and sleepy.

I hadn't noticed.

Tell about how the world isn't as bad as you've made it seem.

Oh but it is.

But you've made it mean and ridiculous. And the people, too.

I apologized in Chapter 51.

Tell about the Normans.

They buy some cookies. They're getting back on the road. Tele-Town . . . I don't know, something about it just doesn't feel right.

Tell about what that one man says to Mr. Norman.

Well, he shakes Mr. Norman's hand and says, We'll be here. He looks him right in the eye and says it. His grip is strong, his skin is tough. There is an openness and a generosity of spirit here that is frankly disturbing. Suspicious.

Tell about Bear v. Shark II.

It should be big. It should be real big.

67

Bear v. Shark:
The Rising Action

At a border town Food Mart just outside of TeleTown, Curtis gets shot by an armed robber. It's not that big a deal—he's been shot before—but still, it's always a little scary.

Curtis is in line to buy some Fruit Roll-Ups when this guy pulls out a gun and tells everyone to drop. Everyone drops, but Curtis is looking at this gun, thinking no way it's real. The thing is *turquoise*.

So his legs are trembling, but he's got this nonchalant look on his face. Sure, he's seen the PSAs—Kids, be smart: if you are unarmed, always obey the commands of armed robbers—but the thing is, Curt has been around the block. He's seen holdups before, hundreds of them. He's made it to the ninth level on *Stick Up!* And it's so embarrassing to get duped, to fall for the old fake gun trick.

And as Matthew and everyone else hits the deck, Curtis is thinking, Look at these rubes. Naive. A bunch of sheep. If this guy told you all to buy Sexy Pants, would you do that, too?

But then the guy turns and shoots Curtis in the arm—the bullet just grazes him, really—before running out of the Food Mart with just a 44 oz. MegaDrink and his turquoise gun.

Curtis says, "I'm fine, really."

An eyewitness says, "That little kid has a certain something that

I've seen numerous times in feature films and also on the expanded tier of my Cable Television Package."

The Food Mart manager says, "In my day, we obeyed gunmen."

A green sign says, "Las Vegas 17."

A scared guy in the locked and filthy Food Mart bathroom says, "I'd kill the family pet for a ticket."

The TeleTown pamphlet in Mr. Norman's shirt pocket says, "We always welcome new members to our unique, self-sustaining community."

Someone on Aisle 6 buys Curtis a box of Band-Aids for being so brave. Matthew puts one on his brother's gunshot wound. The Band-Aid has a robot bounty hunter on it.

Mr. Norman, who has been pacing the parking lot, says, "The problems here are manifold."

After grazing Curtis, the bullet from the turquoise gun detonated a shelf of Road Buddy Canned Hash, and now Curtis can't stop staring at the meaty gore sprayed all over the Food Mart's refrigerated section. He's suddenly gone white, with strands of damp hair stuck to his forehead. While ponytailed camera guys zoom in on the ugly mess in the dairy case, perky news correspondents, materializing from vans and choppers, take turns eliciting one-word answers from the child, who is shaken, Quinn, but unharmed. It could have been kid brains there behind me, Marla, but tonight, thankfully, it is only road hash. Back to you, Brock.

Curtis says, "Dad?"

Mr. Norman says, "You really didn't do the right thing, Curtis."

Curtis says, "Dad?"

Mr. Norman says, "It's like I'm baffled."

Curtis is pale and quivering.

Mr. Norman says, "Come here."

They sit on a sticky bench together outside the Food Mart. It would make a nice shot, but the news crews have already pulled out. Curtis's legs don't touch the ground. Mr. Norman looks at the boy's knees, maybe for the first time ever. They are white, even in August, white and knobby like Insta-Bake Frozen Dinner Rolls. Little knees under shorts.

Curtis says, "Dad?"

Mr. Norman says, "Whisper it in my ear."

Curtis leans up, says, "I don't want to die."

Mr. Norman says, "I know."

Curtis says, "I don't want to die before we get there. To the Darwin Dome."

Mr. Norman says, "I don't want you to die, either."

Curtis says, "I know."

Mr. Norman wonders about farming, he and his boy with hoes, turning the soil, their knees brown and leathery. Crop rotation, fallow fields, seeds.

Mr. Norman says, "We're almost there, pal."

Curtis says, "I have to pee again."

Curtis climbs down from the sticky bench. It's getting dark out.

Mr. Norman says, "Hey, Curt."

Curtis turns around, says, "I know, Dad."

Mr. Norman says, "Let's just say a bear and a shark got in a fight."

Peanuts grow underground. Tiny bugs eat tomato plants.

Curtis giggles, says, "No contest," runs off toward the rest room growling. The sign on the interstate says, "Clean rest rooms," but the thing is, the rest rooms are not clean. They're dirty. The sign is lying.

Mr. Norman, alone on the bench, says, "Who would win?"

Mr. Norman walks to the SUV, where Mrs. Norman and the other son, the older one, are both asleep with headphones on. It's been a long layover at the Food Mart.

Who would win?

Just for argument's sake: A bear and a shark.

Tired and relieved and something else also, Mr. Norman starts the SUV and merges back onto that big road to Vegas.

68

In Superhero-Type Fashion

A Brief History of Twentieth-Century American Culture (Long Story Short ed.)

October 30, 1938: Orson Welles and his Mercury Theater of the Air present a version of Howard Koch's adaptation of H. G. Wells's *The War of the Worlds* in a one-hour radio program. Under Welles's direction, Koch's play is performed as a news broadcast of extraterrestrial invasion. In Koch's adaptation, the high-tech Martian marauders land not in English pastures but in rural New Jersey, and their alien eyes are set on New York City. With heat rays and poison gas, they take thousands of human lives and they advance, Sherman style, upon the most populous city on the planet. The young Orson Welles plays a Princeton astronomer who gives scientific credibility to the whole affair.

Six million people listen to this performance, which is, to modern ears, quite obviously—unmistakably—a performance. An estimated one million people believe that New Jersey has been invaded by Martians, and some of these people take to the streets, firing guns at streetlights and water towers. A few people, faced with a horrible death at the hands of diabolical Martians, attempt to take their own lives.

May 23, 1999: Attached to wires 90 feet above the mat and near the top of the sold-out Kemper Arena in Kansas City, Mo., professional wrestler Owen Hart, thirty-four, is set to make a dramatic entrance into the ring, where he will square off against a WWF foe in yet another grudge match full of myth and mask. The plan, as WWF president Vince McMahon later says, is for Hart to descend in "super-hero-type fashion."

But Hart, his harness incorrectly hitched, plummets 90 feet into the ring. His head hits a turnbuckle and snaps back. He struggles to lift his head and his arms, but then he collapses. Paramedics enter the ring, strip Hart of his trademark Blue Blazer mask, and work unsuccessfully to revive him. He is pronounced dead at the hospital.

Even after Hart's head slams into the metal turnbuckle—an injury that would be, from the perspective of any early-century viewer, unmistakably and horrifically real—many of the 16,200 fans in attendance think the fatal fall is just another of the scripted stunts that have helped make professional wrestling so popular.

Less than twenty-four hours later, 19,000 fans pack the Kiel Center in St. Louis for the next scheduled stop on the WWF tour. The show goes on.

If you enjoyed this LSS edition, look for others on-line. Our catalog includes: Hitler in a Nutshell; The French Revolution, in Essence; The Middle Ages: A Summary; String Theory for the Working Woman; Notes on the Renaissance; Finite Jest; The Pocket Reformation; The Bathroom Einstein; Two-Minute Bible; The Concise Faulkner; and Bear v. Shark: The Novel.

69

A Waterfall

Nearing Las Vegas, Mr. Norman remembers a place that he and his wife used to go together. A place they discovered, a place on his body, actually, this little patch of skin underneath his, you know, his scrotum, that she would touch with fingers or tongue and it was real there and they could go there together. They could mute that old Television, the one he got from his parents, and they could take a trip together to this true place, his soul, the seat of his emotions.

It's Friday night. The industrial sun is setting and it is beautiful.

Without realizing it, Mr. Norman has his hand in his lap, searching for his soul. He can't find it.

When was the last time? Or the last time she bit him? Not hard, ever, just a quick strike, a lunge, lizard-quick. It left a mark and he would cry not because it hurt but just because.

He looks at her and she is sleeping. And she is drooling, I'm afraid.

The President of the United States says, "Well, listen, I think they're both tough competitors, very well matched. Whichever way it comes out, I'm sure it'll be a great fight and I'm sure it'll be great for this nation."

In the rearview mirror Mr. Norman looks back into the darkness. His children are back there somewhere, asleep. He can't see their knees. Mr. Norman wonders if they'll ever get bitten or touched in a way that is true and real.

A reporter says, "Have the authorities taken any steps to prevent the sort of rioting that occurred after Bear v. Shark I?"

Why? Why is he taking his family to Las Vegas?

Las Vegas?

They all need to go somewhere pure, fresh, real. A waterfall, a meadow, a snow-capped mountain. Disneyland, with rides and well-scrubbed youths in costumes and cotton candy and oh Christ no not Disneyland but somewhere else green and fresh with water.

Blue blue blue, a mountain stream, blue as his Web page border, bluer.

The Normans are five miles from the Vegas border.

Melvin in League City, Texas, says, "I'd off my grannie for a ticket. I'd rassle a bear for a ticket. I'd give up my Television for a ticket."

No DVD no DVD no DVD no DVD.

A waterfall. Falling water. He doesn't know, maybe rocks, lichen, snails.

Yes.

He can see it, pure, the water falling down a waterfall.

Mrs. Norman stirs, murmurs.

Yes. Like in that soap commercial.

Mrs. Norman screams.

Mr. Norman exits the interstate. Two left turns and he's back on it, driving away from Las Vegas. Away from the neon horizon, the tits, the gambling, the Spectacle.

and now this . . .

Part Two

Misunderstandings and Their Remedies

70

The Ghost of the American Vacation

Hi, folks, and welcome back to another episode of *American Vacation*. I'm Walt West and next to me here in the studio and providing color commentary for our broadcast this weekend is Chris Blackletter. How'd I do on the name, Chris?

Not too bad, Walt.

Welcome, Chris, and thanks for filling in on such short notice.

I'm happy to be here.

Now Chris, it says here you have a Ph.D. in English from a mid-tier school.

Well, I finished my coursework, Walt.

So you don't actually have a Ph.D.

Not technically.

What did you study?

Rhetoric.

And tell the folks at home a little about rhetoric.

I'm afraid I'm not really very clear on that. After all those books.

A field of study at the nexus between language and reality.

They still haven't found that nexus, Walt. They've given up trying. Damn Holy Grail.

Everything is language.

That's what they say.

So rhetoric is the study of everything.

It appears that way.

So it's really not the study of anything, then, is it?

It doesn't look like it, no.

But you do have a master's degree in English?

Yes.

And that is also from a mid-tier school?

Yes it is.

OK. Good. So Chris, what do you like to do when you're not . . . Well what do you like to do?

I read a lot.

I should hope so!

And I've done some work in the catering business, of course. Which is how you discovered me.

Yeah, nice spread here, by the way. Melon balls, spinach dip, wavy carrots.

We try to interact with both you and the food.

These are good, these bamboo-steamed tofu dumplings. And what's that?

That's an artichoke topiary.

Do you eat it, Chris?

It's more of a decorative type thing.

It's pretty.

And I've freelanced some. I did a piece on cosmetic surgery for this women's business magazine in central North Carolina.

That one got past me, I'm afraid.

My editor seemed to like it.

I bet he did.

She.

She. Say, Chris, you're not a communist, are you?

Well, I'd rather not—

Ha! Just a joke. You're not on trial here, friend.

OK.

Say, if this works out, maybe you can come back and do some more broadcasts this season.

That would be neat, Walt.

Think the boss would let us borrow you again?

Maybe.

Your big break, huh?

Yeah, just lucky for me that Thomas Pynchon couldn't make it.

And David Foster Wallace, Donald Antrim, Lorrie Moore.

Walt, don't forget Rick Moody.

Ooh, yes, he would have been good.

And George Saunders.

OK, so Chris has peed in the cup, it's all official, he's clean as a whistle and we're ready to get started. It looks as if the Normans will hit Las Vegas in ten or fifteen minutes.

Funny how they say clean as a whistle. Your basic whistle has been in people's mouths. Seems like there would be a lot of germs and bugs and stuff on it.

Hey now, that was a colorful thing you just said, Kirk.

Fricky-frack, who needs Pynchon?

Whoa, this is a family show, friend.

Gotcha.

Chris, I know you've done your homework. What are the keys to a successful family vacation this weekend for the Normans?

Well, looking at the children first, Matthew is solid, he's not going to cause many problems. He's surly and jaded, yes. Languid, probably depressive, but he's obedient, you know? But Calvin—

It's Curtis.

But with Curtis, you kind of have to keep your eye on him. He's a weird dude and kind of a mayhem magnet.

Well put.

The kid's probably got an FBI file. Most of his money laundering has been strictly computer gaming, but some of it, apparently, has been real. He tends to get shot.

Yes.

Mrs. Norman is worry free from a viewer's standpoint. She is a great consumer, she's a patriot, she's family oriented, she won't make waves. Somewhere deep in the back of her mind, she may have some reservations about taking her young children to see such gruesome violence, but she isn't about to let these reservations spoil all of the fun. She's excited about the big, bloody show and she just wants to share those moments with her loved ones. And Walt, I'm sure you've noticed, she's just a posture *nut*.

I think probably vitamins are the key to longevity.

It's like whatever happened to the folic acid craze? Here and *gone*.

Chip, what about Mr. Norman?

Walt, Mr. Norman is the wild card here. I think he's the one to watch.

A real loose cannon.

Yes.

A time bomb, huh?

He's been behaving erratically. He's disoriented, exhausted. He daydreams, he babbles. He is nagged by something he cannot name. He doesn't feel connected to anything or anyone. He's lonely, Walt, lonely. He occasionally wonders if this culture has anything of meaning to offer.

Which is sad.

Very.

Because here's a guy who has tickets to what has been called by some the greatest spectacle in all of recorded history.

Bigger than Lincoln-Douglas?

Do you know what people would do for those tickets?

I've heard some of the things, yes.

This Mr. Norman, he's got a job, a family, a Sport Utility Vehicle. He's headed to a country with the best entertainer-to-entertainee ratio in the free world. It's guys like him that really get me, you know? I mean, what more can this guy want?

I'd say maybe he wants a little less.

Any chance you'll finish that Ph.D., Chris?

Doubtful.

Rhetoric is the art of using the available means of persuasion in any given case.

Aristotle.

What I shall urge is that rhetoric should be a study of misunderstandings, and their remedies.

Yeah, I. A. Richards. That's a good one.

The handmaiden to philosophy.

You'll get calls and letters on that one.

So Mr. Norman is the key.

Yeah, he's very unpredictable right now. I just feel like he is capable of anything. Or nothing, maybe. But I guess that's why folks tune in.

Actually, Carl, our research indicates that folks tune in to see average American families enjoying American-style vacations in entertaining pleasure spots.

OK.

And this episode is special because although we're not allowed to broadcast Bear v. Shark, we can broadcast an American family *watching* Bear v. Shark, and for many Americans, this will be as close to the action as they can get.

Did you know, Walt, that my brother-in-law invented Bear v. Shark?

Hey, good one, so did mine!

No really.

It's difficult, Chris, to overestimate the importance of this event to the American public.

No argument there, Walt.

It's a democratizing force.

So I've heard.

With the Internet, everyone with an opinion can have their say and be heard. The poorest squirrel eater out there in the sticks, provided he has a decent Internet provider, can set up his Web page right alongside the rich kid in the suburbs. Technology and entertainment have leveled class distinctions and created a pure form of democracy.

Well.

I mean, what are the chances, one hundred years ago, that these people living out in the wilderness would have ever even heard of bears and sharks? And now they're out there e-gambling, taking part in opinion polls, and talking fins and claws on chat lines. It's staggering how far we've come.

I'm thinking town meeting here, Walt.

Exactly, yes. A town meeting called in a global village to discuss who would win in a fight between two large and fearsome creatures.

Fake creatures.

Well, Chris, fake only in the sense that they are not real.

Granted.

It's palpably galvanizing.

Indeed.

Founding Fathers.

Yes.

Citizenship.

OK.

And *rhetoric,* my friend. In this kind of radically democratic political environment, expertise in rhetoric becomes vital, does it not?

Vital, Walt.

If Joe Six-Pack wants to put his hard-earned money down on either the bear or the shark, he has to be expert in evaluating truth claims and logical coherence.

You're talking here of gambling?

Chris, how do you see the bout?

I'm a shark guy, Walt. I was a shark guy way back when it was just a North Carolina parlor game and I'm still a shark guy. In fact, I've never really understood all the fuss, but I know that there are really smart people who think the bear has the edge.

Yes, as you know, the question does not correlate strongly with education level.

But people in seafaring industries are much more likely to believe the shark will win, and I put some stock in that. Some of these fellas are one-legged, if you catch my drift, Walt.

But the same could be said about folks in the West, the forest rangers and such who rioted after Bear v. Shark I. They're bear people out there. They've seen bears. They know what bears can do. These people have beards and flannel shirts, and they wear the right boots for the job.

Walt, I never really understood how they rioted in the forest.

Overturned trees, looted eagles' nests, that sort of thing.

A civil disobedience situation?

Yes, trashing the forest in the spirit of Thoreau and MLK.

What did that prove, Walt?

It proved that they had strong feelings about something. Rioting is an American tradition. We're a people who riot when we are mad or sad or happy. It was just unfortunate in this case because there were no cameras to capture the spontaneous outburst of feeling. All we have to go on is the rioters' testimony on their Web sites, which are very moving. Rhetorically savvy.

Hey Walt, if a rioter overturns a tree in the forest and nobody— ah, never mind.

Your prediction, Clint?

I like the shark in three rounds. It's going to go longer than the first time, provided they've worked out all the kinks, head size and what have you, but it won't go the distance.

There you have it. I'm Walt West, this is Chris Bandleader, and you're watching *American Vacation,* folks. Say, Chris, did you know that a shark literally cannot swim backward?

That's an urban myth.

Hey Chris, what do you get when you cross a bear and a shark?

I give up.

Mauled.

Well, Walt, you know why the bear lost the first match, don't you?

Umm . . .

He stayed out late the night before looking for a little head.

OK, let's take a look at some of the e-mails we've gotten in the studio from viewers at home. Paul in Ohio writes, *Where's Pynchon. My Internet cable listings said it was going to be Pynchon doing color. That guy with the cummerbund ain't Pynchon.* Well, you can't please everyone, eh Kevin?

I guess not. People get sick. It happens.

OK, Jennifer in New Jersey writes, *I love* American Vacation. *It's way better than* American-Style Journey *and* A Family Trip Situation. *Keep up the good work.* Hey, thanks, Jennifer, it's always nice to get positive feedback.

Thanks, Jennifer.

Nathan in Missouri writes, *Hey whatever happened to Jell-O. It was so huge for a long time and now it's difficult to find and I can't find it. It used to jiggle.* Well, keep looking, Nathan. We've got to take a break now. We'll be right back for more *American Vacation.* Don't touch that dial.

Bad credit? No credit? No problem

and now all of a sudden Turner can't find the strike zone

this administration has clearly shown no interest in the peace talks

we just didn't play with any hunger and they did

her most recent album has soared up the charts

Why they say album?

I dunno. Why they say Don't touch that dial?

another round of successful missile strikes

Nobody has no dial.

human milk is fine for average children

That's what I'm saying.

serial rapist

sleek design

There are guys wearing digital watches in Spartacus, *weren't no digital watches in toga times.*

we recently caught up with the busy little lady in Los Angeles and here's what she had to say

that's the seventh spinal cord injury we've seen this season, Butch

a five-year, 100-million-dollar deal

no word on civilian casualties

last weekend at the box office

high winds

bears can't run downhill

dammit, Billy, you can't just have everything you want life doesn't work like that

meanwhile, the drought continues

you slept with her didn't you well how was she was it worth it

do you have trouble keeping your food down?

Hey flip it back to my show.

What were you watching?

the only hot dog with vitamin C

American Vacation.

the Lord wants you to make sound financial decisions

What channel?

we're so confident that you'll be satisfied that we offer

the blood was actually running down the hill I know you would think that the blood would soak into the earth but what I'm saying is that the ground was so saturated with blood that it ran down the hill and covered our boots

Damn.

Eighty-four, I think.

nobody likes soggy French fries

Shit, eighty-three, then.

If you just joined us, we've got some rather strange news to report. The Normans were just a few miles from the Las Vegas border when Mr. Norman turned the Sport Utility Vehicle completely around.

Total U-turn, Wes.

Walt.

Walt.

I think you'll be able to see the SUV from our aerial cameras. Chris, could you circle it there with the telestrator?

Like so?

No, that's not it. That's a cactus.

Sorry, I don't quite have the hang of this thing.

Yes, that's the one. Right there. Once again, Mr. Norman has turned the four-wheel-drive vehicle around and is heading away from Las Vegas. This is potentially very troubling news, but we don't want to jump to any conclusions. Perhaps they just left some keys or a pair of glasses at a Food Mart somewhere back there.

I don't think so, Walt.

What?

I think it's more serious than that.

But look at how slowly he's driving. Surely if he was trying to make a getaway he would be driving fast, with abandon.

Not necessarily.

Explain. Now's your chance to show your stuff.

Mr. Norman. He's driving. It's . . . He's driving through the slow, falling dark of the desert, away from Las Vegas.

This much is clear from our aerial pictures.

Las Vegas, Walt. Feathered showgirls, relentless Entertainment, gambling in windowless, timeless, placeless mazes where the polychrome flicker and the free drinks and the clatter of impartial machines assaults you, first, then begins to seep into you like novocaine. It's like the outside world. Except louder, more.

Hey now, you got a speech for every city?

There are pictures of winners on the walls, with blank spaces reserved for you: your bloodshot eyes, your wan smile. Funny, winning doesn't feel much different than losing. It's all a rush.

A marvel of human engineering. The art and architecture of it.

Space designed to make you say, over and over, OK, one more time.

It's brilliant, Cyrus.

Away from this place. He is driving away and . . . And night is happening outside his windows, but deliberately. It is not something to be rushed. And maybe a coyote is howling somewhere, maybe a rattler is easing through the sand, maybe a scorpion scuttles into a cowboy's recumbent boot.

The boot, you say, is prostrate.

Help me out, Walt. Are there still scorpions?

Yes, some.

And cowboys?

No. But their boots remain.

And in the dying light the stern silhouettes of cacti line the highway like . . .

Like *dark people*?

No, Walt, like guards, members of some moonlit militia whose duty it is to keep you between the lines.

Foreboding.

And Mr. Norman is driving not recklessly, not feverishly, but slowly, contemplatively, well below the interstate limit. Imagine, Walt, the cool bank robber who bags his money and then walks out the side exit, his walk purposeful, not panicked.

An analogy, yes.

And Mr. Norman feels that high speed, even on this flat and straight and open road, might obliterate thought. Might just blow it away. Mr. Norman imagines a critical velocity—not fixed; generational, perhaps—at which the world rushes by too rapidly for reflection and conjecture.

Today's hectic world not conducive to careful consideration and judgment. OK.

And so the white lines that have all day darted by like bullets or video game missiles or Television news segments are now floating past like logs on a river.

Metaphor.

They're floating past, these white lines, at an almost unlawfully slow rate, Walt.

Fifty-three miles per hour. A thinkin' man's velocity.

And ahead of him Mr. Norman sees the signs and billboards growing larger in discrete units, as if in a slide show or ancient classroom film strip.

I remember those film strips. Demographic studies indicate that most of our viewing audience will understand that trope.

As if magnified to the next power at steady intervals.

Yes.

And behind him, through his rearview mirror, Mr. Norman watches dim and distant vehicles become—through a continuous time-lapse sequence of growth and cell division—bright-eyed monsters of luxury that speed past in a silent roar.

Blastula. Zygote. Next slide.

In a manner of seconds, Walt, embryonic headlights grow to full-sized sedans and then they are gone. This is the world behind him.

Just to catch everyone up to speed, Mr. Norman, just a few miles from the Las Vegas border, turned the Sport Utility Vehicle around and is now heading away from the Entertainment Capital of the World. He's driving slowly, as you can see. Great work, as always, by our *American Vacation* camera crew in the army choppers. I'm Walt West and with me here in his bow tie and providing color commentary is Chris Backacher, a member of the studio's catering team. He has a master's degree in English. Some history of depression and vagrancy and mismanaged affections, but no criminal record, no drugs in his system. A flair, it seems, for the dramatic, perhaps not unlike our Mr. Norman.

I often have a hard time falling asleep.

We know.

As one car passes the Normans' SUV, a small child with a dome-light halo waves and smiles at Mr. Norman.

But Chris, I don't see any cars currently passing the SUV.

By the time Mr. Norman raises his hand in return, the child and the car have vanished into the distant constellation of taillights.

Technically speaking, when does this become a hostage situation?

Mr. Norman loves his children, Walt. You know that, don't you? You *do* know that? At one time this vacation sounded like a good idea. It's just . . .

Are we obligated to call in the National Guard at some point on behalf of the family? I'm thinking rubber bullets here.

He can see those kids in his rearview mirror.

I don't know, Chris, it's pretty dark.

Oh, maybe their dreams make more sense than the world they've been born into.

Those kids have it great, pal. When I was a kid, man oh man.

The radio in the Sport Utility Vehicle is on with the volume turned low. A woman is talking about a product. Mr. Norman cannot hear the words, but he recognizes the intonation of the sell. And maybe this is what it comes down to, not content but form—an Olympian's sleek body, a well-known actress's voice, a jingle, a striking use of color, a fade, a jump-cut, a swish pan, sound effects, a nice ass, innovative text-image placement. Not, Walt, buy *this*. But: *Just buy*. Buy, buy, and we'll all win.

The invisible hand.

The billboards look silly at this speed. They look like a joke. Fake billboards, parodies of themselves. The colorful lies are rhetorically engineered for highway velocity, the quick hit. When you drive too slowly, when you consider the implicit syllogisms—having a fun lifestyle is fun, Hernia Soda leads to a fun lifestyle, and so on—then you are left to believe that advertising is an insult and an absurd waste of money. And also you are left with some vague desire, what is it, an emptiness, a thirst, yes you are thirsty, wouldn't a Hernia Soda hit the spot?

Wow, friend, I find that I'm feeling a little dry myself.

The Vibra-Dream Plus, you must understand, is not female in any literal sense, though its ad campaign has targeted men by using breasts and legs and belly buttons to confuse sexual desire with the desire for comfort after a stressful workday. This kind of confusion happens all the time, Walt. It's good for business. Almost any kind of business.

I hadn't noticed.

The Vibra-Dream Plus, which Mr. Norman wears like a collar, vibrates just audibly, but she does not ever actually say anything.

I understand. Mine never says a word, and that's how I like her.

And Walt, there's his wife in the passenger seat, dozing fitfully.

Can we get a picture of her? There. There's a pretty recent shot of the Mrs.

And Mr. Norman looks over at this person beside him and he feels that certain tenderness you feel for the sleeping and for those whom you no longer love but with whom you share a history. After the rancor or the silence, Walt, can come this hopeless tenderness.

That feels right to me.

And I'm not sure if Las Vegas is technically an independent nation or not, but I'm certain that the Normans have not slept together in months, perhaps a year, perhaps longer. The days just dart past like little tiny fish.

Calendar pages fluttering in the wind like in those old black-and-white movies.

Walt, you can leave the imagery and the Sterno to me.

Because of this breaking news situation, folks, we're not going to cut away to commercial. Please know that the next sixty seconds of broadcast are brought to you by the good people at HardCorp. Hard-Corp: Making life more real for over thirty years.

And even though the desert night is cool, the air conditioner is on and the windows are rolled up in the Sport Utility Vehicle.

We can confirm that, I think.

And in his slightly convex driver's side window, Mr. Norman can see himself, his reflection, by the eerie lights of the high-tech dashboard. It is true that the dashboard is remarkable for the amount of information it conveys. His image tilted and floating like an astronaut or a ghost in the blackening sky above the driver's seat.

HardCorp: Bears, Sharks, and so much more.

There I am, Mr. Norman thinks. There I am, haunting my own journey. The ghost of the American Vacation.

Mr. Norman has increased his speed a bit, but he's well under the limit. I still don't think we've hit a panic situation here. I'm holding out for the possibility of a simpler, less drastic interpretation, not that you haven't been persuasive, if a bit gloomy. Everything I just said and most of what Clem said about ghosts was brought to you by Cereal on a Stick. Cereal on a Stick: Because who has time for hot cereal or cold cereal or a cereal bar?

Cereal on a Stick: Because oatmeal is for giant losers.

That's the spirit, Chris.

So Ockham's Razor is what you're saying, Walt.

I'm just saying maybe you read too much.

You'll see. This isn't about misplaced keys or electronic games. This is about crisis. This is about the human struggle for meaning. This is about a turning point, an awakening. This is about enough is enough.

Off in the distance—can we get a better shot of that?—off in the distance I think—yes, great work, guys, there in the distance you can make out the blue-gray glimmer of TeleTown.

Yes indeed.

Now, Chris. You don't think.

That is precisely what I think.

But why TeleTown? That's hardly an escape.

Maybe, just maybe, TeleTown is not what it seems.

Chris Badchildren is being brought to you today by Chief Executive Orange Juice: The orange juice for the top one percent. CEOJ is not responsible for the opinions expressed in this broadcast.

Not at all what it seems. Maybe the million Televisions are a front. Maybe the million Televisions are not watched.

Chris, you obviously have never tried to not watch a Television that's on.

Maybe Mr. Norman is cutting the old Guardian knot.

It's Gordian.

Maybe the people have come together there in TeleTown for a reason. Maybe they've come together to live a different kind of life. In TeleTown they share the work. In TeleTown there is no money. In TeleTown they farm and the work keeps them strong and healthy. In TeleTown they read books and get together to talk about them.

A utopian community.

Call it what you want.

A bunch of robot zombies. Death of the individual.

In TeleTown, nobody cares about fashion, nobody cares about accumulating stuff. Nobody lives better than anyone else. They cook and bake, play instruments, write, paint, put on plays. It's a thriving artistic community.

No motivation to succeed. Malaise, then bloodshed. The old Dutch decline. If you just joined us, the Normans are fleeing Fun.

In TeleTown the Normans can perhaps remake their lives and reestablish their familial relationships. They can cultivate real friendships. You know, there was one Christmas a long time ago when Mr. and Mrs. Norman made each other gifts. It was a little rule they had. And the gifts were pretty good, too, and they meant a lot. Why did they stop doing that?

Any republication, rebroadcast, or retransmission of the events, images, or descriptions of this telecast without express written consent of *American Vacation* is strictly prohibited.

I'm not saying it's perfect in TeleTown. These are humans we're talking about. There are arguments about how things are, how things should be. But there is a basic, shared commitment to justice and fairness.

I think that guy over there needs your bottle opener.

TeleTown, Walt. TeleTown.

Chris, what do you think the rest of the Norman family is doing in that vehicle? Surely someone would have woken up and noticed the change in direction.

There is confusion and anger. You have to expect this. The boys, especially Curtis, are upset. Mrs. Norman doesn't want to take sides, but she wishes Mr. Norman hadn't turned around. She says, Honey?

She says, Maybe we should talk about this. Curtis says, I hate your guts, Dad. He says, You're ruining my life. And Matthew, maybe Matthew says, Shit, it's not like the cookies are even that good.

There are certain words. From a family-style perspective.

Curtis says, Let me out of this car, I hate you, you're a bastard fucker.

It's those kinds of words.

This stings, of course, but Mr. Norman keeps driving. You'll see, he says. I promise it will be better where we're going. I promise. Mrs. Norman maybe cries quietly. She is torn. She wants to believe him, but it's true he's been acting strangely.

Interesting, but all speculative, of course.

No, it's true, Walt.

Whoa, what's that up ahead, in the median? Can we get a closer shot of that?

It will be difficult for the Normans. It's never an easy transition.

Is that a . . . ? It looks like it may be a person.

It's happened before. A family comes to TeleTown and they can't all adjust. It's hard work.

Up ahead in the median, there, it's a person. A very small person. Looks like a child.

Imagine trying to wean people of Television in a community full of Televisions. It doesn't always work. People come and then leave. Sometimes families even split up.

It *is* a child, a boy, walking down the median in the direction of the Normans' vehicle. The Sport Utility Vehicle is about a half mile from the child and it is slowing down. Now what do you make of this, Chris?

In TeleTown Mr. Norman will be reborn. He will start to feel again. He's been numb for years. He will cry and laugh. He will discover that he has talents he never knew about.

Is that Curtis Norman?

He will have very few possessions. He will feel light.

My word, that *is* Curtis Norman in the median. How about that? The Sport Utility Vehicle is slowing, slowing on the interstate, and now it is pulling over into the median. It has come to a stop. How did they manage to leave that kid behind?

I just don't know if Mr. Norman's wife and his two children will be ready for the change. You have to be ready. Maybe they will leave immediately to make it back to Vegas for Bear v. Shark. Maybe they will stay a week, a month, a year. Maybe they will adjust, but it is more likely that they will not. They will miss their Internet and their violent movies. Mr. Norman will have to make a choice—will he remain in TeleTown or will he leave with his family?

Curtis has now climbed into the Sport Utility Vehicle. Well, I guess you were right, Clyde, it wasn't about misplaced keys or video games.

And Mr. Norman wandering the clean dirt paths of TeleTown. He has an awful choice to make. It's after midnight. The blue-gray fog is thick and it is a reminder of his former life. Entertainment exhaust. Beautiful but of no substance.

Mr. Norman is turning the vehicle around in the median. It looks like . . . yes, he's turning the Sport Utility Vehicle around once more. The Normans are back on the interstate, heading toward Las Vegas. They're picking up speed, they're really moving. Wow, what a strange turn of events, so to speak.

A lone man down in a canyon, wandering the dusty makeshift roads as interstate travelers rush past overhead. Through the blue-gray haze he sees the flashing white lights of nighttime photographers. Everyone wants a shot of the TV ghetto, the scenic bivouac. He never drives a car anymore and he has grown to hate the speed and swoosh up above. If he gets back on that interstate, Walt, he feels that he will be destroyed.

Chris—

He doesn't want to go where it leads. It's no place for living, up there. His immune system could no longer handle such sweetness, such loudness, such brightness. The quick images would crush him and break his heart a hundred times a day, the endless chatter would be a mosquito in his ear all day and all night. And yet, who can just send away a family? He loves those boys. He—

Chris. Chris, hate to cut you off there, pal, some of that stuff was pretty good, but the situation is over. The family disaster has been averted.

What?

Normans heading back to Vegas. Cruise control, 76 miles per hour. Folks, the little Norman boy in the median was brought to you by Green Paint.

But the life ahead.

Bear v. Shark. An exciting weekend of broadcasting.

It can't be.

Take a look for yourself. Monitor three, over there.

Ah *Jesus*.

And when you get a chance, the boys in production would love some more of those little chicken fingers.

and now this . . .

Part Three

Las Vegas

71

The Brutal Engine of History

Just about twenty hours until Bear v. Shark II:
Red in Tooth and Claw.
Natural Enemies Square Off in the Darwin Dome.
Lungs v. Gills in the Neon Desert for All the Marbles.
Realer than Life.
Shark and Bear Collide in Dog-Eat-Dog World.
Witness the Brutal Engine of History in State-of-the-Art Comfort.
Flight Is Not an Option.
Raw Instinct in Incredible Three-Dimensional Projection.
The Struggle for Existence Inevitably Follows from the High Geo-
metrical Ratio of Increase Which Is Common to All Organic Beings!
The Bear Is Back and This Time His Head Won't Be So Small!
This Ain't Personal. It's Genetic.
The Flag May Be at Half-Mast, but the Action Will Be Full Tilt.
Savage, Bone-Crushing Fun for the Entire Family.

72

At the Border

The Normans are stopped at the Las Vegas border. Routine check. The country's distant skyline looks bright and fun.

Why are you coming to Las Vegas?

To witness History.

How long will you be staying here?

Just until Sunday.

Mind if we have a look in the vehicle?

No.

Hey, is that Curtis Norman in the backseat?

Yes.

Hi, Curtis.

Hi.

How you feeling?

Fine.

The border station is lit up brighter than day. Choppers fly overhead. Minimum-wagers hang from wires and announce hotel specials with bullhorns.

A border official says, "Sorry for the inconvenience, but we need to search everybody coming in this weekend. You wouldn't believe how many people have it in mind to blow up the Dome."

Mrs. Norman says, "That's just awful."

The border official says, "It just seems like these days, whenever you have people getting together to have a good time, you can bet there's somebody out there who wants to detonate the fun."

The Normans step out of the vehicle. A border guard approaches Mr. Norman and asks him to come fill out some paperwork in his car. He (the guard) has a cool uniform, better than normal cops in America.

Mr. Norman says, "Paperwork?"

The border guard says, "Uh, yes, just some routine documents." His eyes look weird and Mr. Norman thinks perhaps he is not telling the truth. Maybe this is a trap. The guard is wearing a hat with a long feather in it.

Mr. Norman can picture his tiny Las Vegas prison cell. Two meals a day. Cabbage, a lot of cabbage. Tepid water. Bread so hard it hurts to chew. A small bed in the corner with a caved-in mattress, a rust-stained sink, a toilet. The days like a long picket fence scratched into the wall. Stack of paperbacks by the bed, some notebooks. He would write in the notebooks. He would fill them up with something. His thoughts. Surely if he were in prison he'd have some thoughts. About life on the Inside. Life on the Outside. Body shackled but mind free. Sent upriver. The hoosegow.

The sky says, "Indoor pool, kitchenettes, free movie channels."

Neil Postman says, "Today, we must look to Las Vegas as a metaphor of our national character and aspiration."

Mr. Norman accompanies the border guard to the patrol car. It's an El Camino. They get in and the border guard offers Mr. Norman a cigarette. Mr. Norman declines, but then immediately thinks about how important cigarettes will be in the clink. The slammer.

The border guard blows smoke out the window. He says, "Sir, I overheard you saying that you are going to the show tomorrow night." His accent doesn't sound that much different from the folks in the Mainland.

Line by line Mr. Norman would fill up those notebooks using pencils sharpened with a contraband pocket knife. And oh the conjurer visits, don't think he doesn't know what goes on.

The border guard says, "I speak to you now, sir, not as an officer of the law with the authority to arrest and shoot people, but as a man. As a father. Father to father."

They provide your uniforms. You don't have to keep track of keys or remote controls or lost children. You could just sit there in that cell and really think and live. Hundreds of push-ups a day to build up the chest and arms.

The border guard says, "Sir, I have a little crippled boy at home that I raise all by myself. My wife has expired."

Mr. Norman cannot think of a single crime that he can confess. He's done nothing wrong. He's clean, heartbreakingly clean. He pissed in the pool at the Plugged Inn, big deal. There are no bombs in the Sport Utility Vehicle. Not one single bomb.

Overhead the humming sky says, "King-size beds, children under 10 eat free."

A banner says, "Las Vegas: All the fun of America with none of the news."

The border guard's hat feather is pressed flat and pretty against the red ceiling of the El Camino. He says, "Doctors say my crippled boy may have about a year or two left. That's all. Now, sir, do you know what my son—Reggie's his name—do you know what Reggie wants more than anything else in this world?"

Mr. Norman says, "To live?"

The border guard blows smoke. He says, "Well, that goes without saying."

Mr. Norman says, "To walk?"

The border guard says, "More than anything else in this world he wants to go to Bear v. Shark."

Mr. Norman looks wistfully at the border guard's handcuffs.

The sky says, "Free shuttle service to the Dome."

The border guard says, "Now, I am prepared to make you a generous offer for two tickets."

The border guard pulls a pen from his cape and writes a figure on a scrap of paper. He hands Mr. Norman the scrap. Mr. Norman holds the scrap up to the window. Generous, indeed. We're talking about an addition to the house or a couple semesters of college for one of the boys.

Mr. Norman looks over at his vehicle, which is now parked on Las Vegas soil. It's not soil, really. More like Astroturf, brilliant green stubble under the lights. Border officials are searching the Sport Utility Vehicle. They won't find a damn thing. Mrs. Norman stands to the side, working on an electronic quilt. The boys are running on the turf, throwing rocks at each other. They are shouting, keeping score. It's some type of bear/shark spin-off game, the rules seem simple enough.

God, or a dangling teen, says, "Slots in your room."

Mr. Norman turns back to the border guard. He says, "Listen, I'd like to help you, but I can't."

The border guard says, "Rodney is crippled."

Mr. Norman says, "It's Reggie, and I'm sorry. Really I am. But I'm on a vacation with my family."

Matthew says, "Three-zip, bear-lover."

The border guard says, "Reggie doesn't have long. It's all he wants."

Mr. Norman opens his door and puts a leg out of the car. He says, "There's always PayView."

Curtis says, "That one hit my neck."

The border guard says, "It's a sad fucking day when a little crippled boy with a month to live can't go see a bear and a shark fight each other."

73

The Worst Kind of People

Most people will answer "bear" or "shark" very quickly and then proceed to provide reasons. You've heard most of these reasons by now. The fins, the teeth, the mammalian brain, the hibernation factor, energy fields, color blindness, eyeball rays, the shark tongue.

Etc.

There are very few fence-sitters, and there is very little apathy. And it's rare that someone takes time to consider the question and weigh the evidence. Seldom do people change their minds, though it's been known to happen. It seems to be a gut thing. The answer just feels right and then you come up with reasons.

But there are some people, and you know the type, who refuse to answer until they have, say it with me now, *more information*. They say things like, "Well what kind of shark are we talking about and what kind of bear?" They say, "Hammerhead v. Grizzly is a whole different ball game from Great White v. Polar or Sand v. Brown or Tiger v. Koala." And they say, "And how deep is the water, *exactly,* and is it fresh water or salt water?" And worst of all: "Why would they ever fight? They have different ecological niches and they don't share the same food supply. A bear's digestive system blah blah blah."

God I hate these people.

Matthew hates these people, too.

If you run into someone like this, just make your way quickly to a different part of the parlor. These are the people you have to look out for. These are the people who—well, it's like they're terrified that someone somewhere might be having fun.

74

Festive,
Jubilant Atmosphere

XIX hours until Bear v. Shark II.

The lobby of the Normans' hotel looks even better in person than on the Internet. Except there are no exotically hued fish in the huge aquarium behind the front desk.

Mrs. Norman says to the front desk person, "Where are the colorful fish?"

The front desk person says, "They died."

Mrs. Norman says, "Oh."

The front desk person, who is wearing a sexy toga, says, "It happens."

Mrs. Norman says, "Part of the life cycle."

The front desk person says, "It happens every few months. These fish can't seem to survive in our tank for very long. So they die off and so we just order new ones. People want to see the colorful ones."

Mrs. Norman says, "Sure."

The front desk person gives Mrs. Norman the keys and gives Curtis a T-shirt.

Curtis says, "Thanks."

Mrs. Norman says, "It could be ich or dropsy."

The T-shirt says, "I won the Bear v. Shark essay contest and you didn't."

Mr. Norman sits in the crowded lobby. There are crumbling columns and wax gladiators. Chariots race and slaves battle to the death for a fruit-eating emperor in a gigantic ceiling mural.

Everyone looks familiar. Did he see them in TeleTown? At a Food Mart in America? In the small Television lounge of the Plugged Inn? Are they stars of Comedies, either romantic or situation? Are they the vixens and cads of Prime Time that we love to hate? Is that his family over there at the front desk?

There are supposed to be many stars in Vegas this weekend.

Banners say, "Welcome Bear Fans & Shark Fans."

Some guy whose T-shirt says, "Lindbergh is a lie," says, "Glad to see you here."

Some other guy says, "I'll meet you later."

In the corner of the lobby, two grown adults gallop violently on Plexiglas horses in a horse-racing video game. The loser says, "I got gypped."

A crying person says, "I just can't believe I'm actually here. I cannot believe it. I cannot believe it."

A Television Reporter for an American station stares into a camera and says, "Here in the lobby of the Roman Coliseum, there is a festive, jubilant atmosphere."

A Television in the corner says the same thing at the same time.

The losing guy on the Plexiglas horse leans back, out of breath. He says, "That fucking sucks."

Mr. Norman asks a pretty woman for her autograph.

The pretty woman smiles and says, "I don't think I'm who you think I am."

Mr. Norman says, "Who are you?"

The pretty woman says, "I'm just a pretty woman."

Mr. Norman says, "That's who I thought you were."

The pretty woman autographs a Food Mart receipt up against an Automatic Teller Machine (ATM) shaped like a slave-eating lion.

Someone says, "I'm telling you, the shark looked puffy and pale."

Mrs. Norman and the boys make their way through the crowd to Mr. Norman and the pretty woman. Mrs. Norman says to the pretty woman, "You look familiar."

The front desk person says, "The new fish are on order, sir. There's nothing we can do about it."

The horse-racing loser pushes the horse-racing winner off his Plexiglas horse. The winner falls and his elbow bends the wrong way.

A banner says, "Las Vegas: America's younger, good-lookin' sister."

75

Bear v. Shark: The Logo

A woman in an office says:

The official logo for Bear v. Shark I, we felt, was all wrong. The shark was cartoony. You can see here—the big, toothy smile and the waving fin. I'm just not thinking *ravined* here. This image gives no sense of the shark's ability to make the sea boil with blood. And the bear? Well, take a look. Way too Soviet. A stern profile that expresses the animal's strength adequately but really fails to capture the bear's natural charisma or its fun-loving disposition. Bears are in circuses, after all. They dance and ride tiny bicycles.

The challenge, really, was to convey the split personalities of these beasts, and that's what our firm tried to do for the Bear v. Shark II official logo. What we have here are two animals who are both a great deal of fun, and yet also are killing machines who rip meaty limbs from torsos. You want to scare kids, but you don't want to scare them *too* much, you know what I mean? It's got to say Nature *and* Vegas. Moreover, you want to make it appear evenly matched. You don't want to make it seem like you are rooting for one over the other. This isn't so easy.

I don't mind telling you that I'm really tickled at the way it came out. I think our artists did a fantastic job. And the color scheme—the charcoal gray with the cadmium yellow—strikes me as a perfect way to represent these complicated and beautiful creatures.

76

Like the Dial of a Radio

A smooth, bright elevator, then a fluorescent corridor.

The Normans walk through a long hallway on the twenty-first floor of the Roman Coliseum.

Televised people on boxes within boxes laugh or cry convincingly, and the muffled sounds are a comfort to the road-weary family. Outside of almost every door they hear a voice they recognize. Walking the hallway is like turning the dial of a radio—God, do you remember radio dials?—or like channel surfing in three-dimensional space. Ball game? Take about ten steps back. A very funny and occasionally touching syndicated Situation Comedy about a group of cool friends who hang out together in a thick stew of sexual tension? All the way to the end of the hall. The advertisements—the jingles, the catchwords, the 25% mores and 50% lesses—seep out into the hallway and infiltrate desire.

Ever seen ants on something dying or dead?

Is a dead mouse really still a mouse?

It's been a long day and it's late. Mrs. Norman's posture frankly just isn't what it was when she started this trip.

Matthew says to Curtis, "By the way, what happened to you back there in America?"

Curtis says, "I got up briefly with this cult."

Matthew says, "What was the cult's belief system?"

The hallway carpet says, "All roads lead to Fun!"

Curtis says, "Essentially, they believe that the bear and the shark are like the Trinity. It's a complicated ideational grid."

Matthew says, "Sounds stupid."

Mrs. Norman says, "Matthew, beliefs cannot be right or wrong. We need to tolerate and respect all systems of thought, no matter how stupid or bankrupt they are."

Curtis says, "I didn't quite catch all the nuances, but it turns out they want to blow up the Dome."

Matthew says, "Well get in line."

The hotel room doors say, "MMCXII . . . MMCXIV . . . MMCXVI . . . MMCXVIII."

Trays of half-eaten meals lie on the floor outside the doors.

A Televised Person says, "I'm feelin' like a bitch in heat!"

The audiences laugh: (1) The live studio audience before which the show was taped; (2) the lonely person locked inside the hotel room; (3) the children walking through the hall.

Curtis says, "That's the one where Alex thinks he's in bed with Lola, but it's really David's mother."

Matthew says, "That one's OK."

The signs on all the doors say, "Do Not Disturb."

Mr. Norman knows that you can be so damn tired and still not be able to fall asleep.

The hotel hallway stretches on and on.

77

Some Common
Freshwater Diseases

Just *try* to keep a real pretty fish healthy. There ain't no doin' it.
Not hardy creatures.

Turn sideways like *that*.

Brilliant scales get all fuzzy and rotted.

Among the thousand natural shocks are Ammonia Poisoning,
Black Spot, Corneybacteria.

Dropsy, Fungal Infection.

Velvet, Ich.

Parasitic Infestation.

The symptoms of your Ammonia Poisoning include red or bleeding gills.

Fish tend to get darker in color and they gasp for air at the surface.

Their very home is a poisonous cage.

Can be prevented but not cured.

Avoid adding expensive fish to new tanks.

Just makes sense, don't it?

Start with cheap fish.

Canaries in the coal mine.

Splurge and get yourself an ammonia detoxifier.

I think the symptoms of Black Spot go pretty much without
saying.

Tends to strike your Silver Dollars and your Pariahs.

Corneybacteria leads to a swollen head that will inevitably push the eyes outward.

Pop 'em right out in some rare and severe cases.

With Dropsy you can expect bulging sides and stomach.

Dropsy is not technically a disease. It's a symptom, a common one.

With your Fungal Infections keep on the lookout for a cottonlike substance on the fins and mouth.

There are many fine commercially available products to cure Velvet, a very common disease that has something to do with pustules.

You want to handle Ich?

What can I say? Watch for white pimply fins.

Treatment of Ich can be difficult.

With your Parasitic Infestation, you got to lay hands on the colorful host in question. You got to physically remove the visible worms, flukes, or lice.

Follow with commercially available treatment such as AquaTech's Fluke-B-Gone or Parasite Armageddon by Trident Laboratories.

All this information is on the Net.

Or write for a transcript.

78

Bear v. Shark: The Cone

The question is absurd, as are most profound questions:

Given a relatively level playing field—i.e., so that the water doesn't run off—enough water so . . . Wait, shit, how's it go?

Something about dexterity.

OK. Given a level body of water—not so much water that the bear has to breathe underwater but not such a little bit that the shark would just be flailing around like a beached whale.

With dexterity.

Yes, with dexterity. Given this and with the water perfect and everything, who would win if a shark and a bear got into a fight.

A bear and a shark.

Right, a bear and a shark, who would win in a fight if they got in one.

The question is apparently of Ancient Eastern extraction.

Yes right a cone but except also I heard it might not be that.

79

Noble Gas

The hotel room is, well, nice. All expenses paid, too. And it's like the essay wasn't really all that well written. Not bad, but not fantastic. Besides that, the part about the Dutch gardener was just simply fabricated. The Normans don't have a gardener, Dutch or otherwise. I can verify that.

So it's a lie. Bold-faced or bald-faced is it? Little white?

Transgression or poetic license?

Should the Normans give their tickets back?

That was a joke.

The view from the window, particularly if you enjoy neon, is extraordinary.

The Darwin Dome stutter-glows in the distance.

The shower cap in the bathroom says, "One size fits most."

Neon is a gaseous element occurring in small amounts in the earth's atmosphere. It's *all natural* is what I'm saying.

Someone, probably a parent, says, "Tomorrow is a big day." This means it's time for bed, even though there are plenty of good Television programs on. The Televisions can stay on, it's not like they turn off, but let's turn the volume down a bit and let's try to sleep, OK? The Televisions are here for you, sweethearts, they're not going anywhere. They'll be here when you wake up, brush your teeth, that's it, you want to be well rested tomorrow night when the land meets the sea.

Mr. Norman.

He watches some Vegas Television, it's anthropological work. What does this culture value? What is taboo here? What kind of people are considered important or worthy? Who has power? What is considered funny?

Hell, it looks about the same as American-style programming. Maybe a little racier. We live in a melting pot. Cultural distinctions fade away, especially where there are no geographical boundaries.

When Las Vegans refer to their homeland as the "Island of Good Times," they are of course speaking metaphorically.

To the extent that cultural differences linger, we must respect and tolerate them.

She (the Vibra-Dream Plus) says, "You just might be Father of the Year."

Neon (Ne) comes from the Greek, meaning "new" or "recent."

Neon—with helium, argon, krypton, xenon, and radon—is a noble gas.

New and noble, what's not to like?

Mr. Norman cannot sleep. His eyelids flutter open when he tries to close them. In his head the words dart and collide like heated-up electrons. Protons or whatever.

He says, "If your neck isn't beautiful, then why even bother?"

He says, "When life throws you a curve, make lemonade."

Mrs. Norman is indeed lovely when she sleeps.

Mr. Norman gets out of bed and gets dressed. Neon's atomic number is 10 and its atomic weight is 20.183.

She (the pillow) says, "Where are you going? No, don't leave. Please don't. Nothing good can come of this."

Another name for the noble gases is inert gases. Inactive or sluggish by nature. Unable to combine with anything else.

Who knows, maybe if Mr. Norman had tried a little harder, he could have fallen asleep. There's always *what if*.

Mr. Norman quietly leaves the hotel room and here's the thing: His youngest boy, Curtis, sees him leave and follows him. A little father-son outing.

80

Undercard

An electronic form letter mailed from Las Vegas officials to Internet cult leaders and remnant Folksingers says:

Dear zealots:

If you are thinking of trying some "funny business" on August 18 here in Las Vegas, you might want to think again.

First of all, security is tight at the border, on the streets, and in the Dome. As of this early date, we have already apprehended many would-be terrorists. Those clever fertilizer artists, the ones still alive, are now eating cabbage and rotting away in a prison with a pretty severe TV-to-prisoner ratio. Ain't no summer camp, I'll tell you.

Second, let me remind you that here in Las Vegas, we don't share the same judicial values as your fair-minded Mother Country. We make no claims to due process, jury of one's peers, speedy trial, etc. We shoot on suspicion. We are prone to hysteria and vengeful thoughts. Extradition from Las Vegas to America tends to be a difficult process. Some of the boys here in law enforcement think that a public execution might be a nice undercard to the big bout in the Dome. A doubleheader. Let's play two.

Here in L.V. we don't care what you do out there in your sprawling nightmare of a nation. You don't bother us, we don't bother you. We're neutral. We're the damn Swiss of the desert. So go ahead and blow up whatever you want on your turf, hell, it certainly can't hurt anything. But let's keep Las Vegas beautiful.

81

Wheel of Sin and Fun

Midnight, eighteen hours until Bear v. Shark II.

Mr. Norman, down twenty-one floors, out on the street. It's all narcotics, hookers, and inert gas out here.

Cops are rounding up homeless entertainers. Some of them (entertainers) are quite talented, just never caught a break.

An entertainer bum says, "We've been out here for months."

A cop hits him on the knee with a sequined club. He (the cop) says, "But we want our country to look nice on American Television, don't we?"

A large truck backs up slowly to a loading dock at the Roman Coliseum. Many of the colorful fish inside the truck already have pustules and swollen heads. Some are gasping for air. Their gills bleed in the dark, splashing water.

Mr. Norman starts walking, he can't imagine that one direction is much different from any other direction. Curtis follows at a distance like a gumshoe. A private dick. It's like that computer game where you have to follow slouching agents of evil and then stab them with a poison umbrella before it's too late.

An assisted-living community explodes in the distance.

A hooker says, "I love the babbling type."

Another hooker says, "Inertia makes me hot."

There are people everywhere and cop cars and lights and vomit.

Smutty handbills line the streets and sidewalks, marking zigzag paths to iniquitous places. These paths fan out in every direction like wavy spokes on a giant wheel. A nation-sized wheel of sin and fun.

Mr. Norman isn't looking where he's going, not looking for the action. He figures he will be found. He figures the action will come to him. He figures choosing a direction is like choosing a channel. Now you just sort of sit back and watch what happens.

A hand on his shoulder, a whisper in his ear, the faint scent of fertilizer.

Mr. Norman says, "What?"

A voice says, "It's no way to live."

A voice says, "Join us."

A voice says, "The boy can come, too."

The throbbing sky says, "Free shower caps."

Mr. Norman says, "What boy?"

Curtis says, "Hi, Dad."

Father and son duck furtively out of the street and into a hotel lobby.

Once you stab the guy with the umbrella, you steal his dossier and double-time it to the docks to get your next assignment.

82

Answer Key

1. **False.** The shark does in fact have a tongue, known as a basihyal, though it does not much resemble the muscular, useful, and mobile slab in the human mouth, or in the mouths of other non-fish vertebrates (such as the bear). The basihyal, a stout and stationary piece of cartilage, lies small and useless on the floor of the shark's mouth.

2. **True.** Some polar and Kodiak bears stand over nine feet tall and weigh in at 1,600 pounds or more. These animals are the largest meat-eating creatures on land (and they can still run a lot faster than you!).

3. **False.** Sharks have excellent vision and they see well at night. Shark corneas have even been transplanted into humans. Sharks also hear very well and have an excellent sense of smell. Also, did you know that sharks have a sixth sense? They can detect vibrations in the water with a special electroreceptive organ.

4. **False.** While it is true that most bears are omnivorous, the koala bear is not a bear at all, but a marsupial.

5. **True.** These pups are generally 40–50 cm at birth.

6. **True.** That's like eating 42 hamburgers a day!

7. **True.** While a 59-foot whale shark has been reported, most tend to be 25–30 feet.

8. *Very* **False.** Sharks go back over 400 million years; bears about 40 million.

9. **False.** Sharks, like almost all other fishes, have no auguring ability.

10. **True.** In Korea, a bear's gallbladder was once sold for $55,000.

11. **False.** On average, one human is killed every year in a shark attack. Most shark attacks are not fatal. Sharks don't much seem to like the taste of humans, who have a much lower fat content than the tasty seal.

12. **True.** The digestive system of hibernating bears is specially designed to process waste internally.

83

A Force for Cultural Cohesion

Mr. Norman (father) and Curtis (son) in a dark and crowded third-floor hotel room in Las Vegas. Middle of the night. Murmuring and plotting. A cult HQ.

An overconfident cult member says, "Ha, I've seen better security in elementary schools."

Mr. Norman says, "How did you follow me here?"

From what Mr. Norman can make out, the members of this cult love and live for Bear v. Shark. And that is why they must destroy it with bombs. This makes sense, does it not? They prefer to be in a continuous and acute state of anticipation and desire. They love the speculation, the wagering, the Talk Radio. They love the chat sites and the swirling rumors and the merchandise. To honor Bear v. Shark and to love it purely is to defer it eternally, to place it forever out of reach. They must want and they must not get what they want. They must not, for what is on the other side?

The Vice Squad Leader in the hotel lobby says, "We hit them quick and we hit them hard."

Listen, after Bear v. Shark I, there was widespread depression and anomie. Suicide rates went up. Spousal abuse rates and homicide rates went up. School dropout rates went up. It's like the whole damn country of America fell apart. What was left? Some boring war, game shows, the Super Bowl.

This cult in question, this cult that Mr. Norman and his young son have more or less joined for the moment, this cult sees itself as a positive force, a force for cultural cohesion and unity. The power of a well-made and well-placed bomb. Funny how you need to destroy to preserve, but you do. You need to blow something up to keep something much larger and more important intact. This is the truth, can you argue with it?

Curtis is struggling with this concept, you can see it in his young face. Delayed gratification is for adults and sickos. And eternally delayed gratification is an austere and ascetical code indeed. Struggle is not fun. Nor is it particularly healthy. Boredom always looms.

Does he (Curtis) love Bear v. Shark?

Yes.

Well, then.

But.

My child, do you or do you not love Bear v. Shark?

I *do*.

Then you must not be selfish. Your place is with us.

The Vice Squad Leader is real, not televised. He says, "We knock. If they don't open up, then we're going in."

It's dark in the room. One lamp on, in the corner, with a towel draped over it. Mr. Norman is not certain that he loves Bear v. Shark, but this feels right to him somehow. He wishes Curtis had not trailed him, but perhaps it will be a good thing, after all. Things usually turn out OK.

The cult members spread out a detailed map of the Darwin Dome on a king-size bed. Certain key places are marked in red.

One cult member in a dark corner says, "Those Lindberghers are *total* wackos."

One cult member in another dark corner says, "So a Panda, an American Black, and an Asiatic Black walk into a bar."

The Vice Squad Leader knocks on the door.

The Cult Leader says, "Who is it?" Terrible falsetto.

The Vice Squad Leader says, "The maid." Better, but hardly convincing.

A cult member in a corner says, "Then the Panda says, 'Give me a rum and Coke.'"

The Cult Leader says, "Come back tomorrow."

The Vice Squad breaks down the door and rushes into the room, looking every bit as well trained and proficient as your typical Television Vice Squad.

A gun says, "Bang."

Another gun says, "Bang."

Mortally wounded Cultists and Vice Officers converse in a gargling pidgin of pain.

Mr. Norman and his boy roll out onto the patio. Curtis hides behind a plastic chair. Mr. Norman climbs over the railing and then jumps three stories to the Astroturf. He tries to roll upon impact like Television leapers do. The turf burns his arms.

Mr. Norman says, "Jump, Curtis."

He says, "Jump, quick."

He says, "I'll catch you."

Curtis climbs on top of the thin railing and stands up. Bullets are whispering in the night. They fly over him, beside him, between his plump white legs.

It's like this kid is invincible.

And he's smiling, too, he's having fun, he loves his old man, Father of the Year, they're having a night on the town. Is he smiling, this boy on the balcony?

Curtis says, "I can't do it."

Mr. Norman says, "Jump, Curtis."

Curtis says, "I'm scared."

Mr. Norman says, "It's OK."

Curtis jumps like a scuba diver jumps into the ocean, a shark hunter perhaps, fins first, and here's the thing: on his way down he smashes the back of his head against the balcony's cement ledge and he crumples, midair, and he falls limp into his father's waiting arms.

An eyewitness, in town for the big show over at the Dome, says, "That was cool."

84

Shark's Tongue

I did OK, seven out of ten.

Me, too.

But I feel like the shark's tongue question is controversial.

How so?

I feel like the question should either be thrown out, giving me seven out of nine, or I should get credit for my answer, which would give me eight of ten.

It's not that big a deal.

It's just the principle of the thing.

What principle are you invoking here, specifically?

It's just a saying.

But still, there's some specific principle.

Principle of the thing, people say that all the time. It's the principle of the thing.

Sure, but there's still some principle they're talking about.

Well. Fairness, then. Or justice.

Why is the tongue question unjust?

Can of worms here involving demarcation, definition. Bee in the thinking man's bonnet for all times.

What's a tongue, you mean.

Yeah, I mean, you start taking legs off a chair, when does it cease and desist being a chair?

At what point.

Likewise, you sit on a flat rock, is the rock now a chair?

Various schools of thought. Natural kinds and whatnot.

Does our language name reality or does it bring reality into being.

But stubby cartilage in mouth floor is a tongue for realists and nominalists alike.

Not necessarily.

I got that one right, No. 1.

They don't even call it a tongue. They say, what, basihyal.

Your proposal would leave me with either six out of nine or six out of ten. That sucks.

And, also, this basihyal doesn't move or anything. Just sits there, useless. Take a tongue out of my mouth and I'll miss it, you can be sure of that.

People live without tongues.

The word *tongue* has to point to something. A tongue has properties. Location and function. Not just any oral lump or knob can be a tongue. The word then loses any referential power whatsoever.

I find that I'm OK with the question as it stands.

85

Thirty Thousand Teeth

Seventeen hours until Bear v. Shark II, we got ourselves an injured child.

These things usually turn out OK.

What they do is build up the suspense and then show you a bunch of commercials and then they come back and everything turns out OK, and there you were, worried for nothing. Or else, worst-case scenario, they give you a cliffhanger and you have to wait, but then when you join them the following week, everything turns out OK, triumph of the human spirit.

A homeless entertainer in the street says, "What that kid has is a fractured skull and swelling on the brain."

Another homeless entertainer, a fine pianist in his prime, says, "Nah, what that child has is a bump on his noggin, no biggie."

I looked it up, the Internet says there are 250 species of sharks and it also says there are 345 species of sharks and also 400 species of sharks. Now dammit, which one is it?

Mr. Norman carrying ragdoll Curtis along the streets of Las Vegas. Mr. Norman can't figure out if he feels, carrying his young boy in his arms, like a good father or a very bad father. Mostly bad.

A drunk motorist says, "Hey, did you win that kid at a gaming table?"

Another drunk motorist says, "Hey, is that little boy sleepy or dead?"

The inert gas twinkles and shines. It's either beautiful out here on the street in Las Vegas, or else it's ugly. Horrid.

Curtis says nothing, but he's still breathing, let's be clear about that.

An entertainer bum says, "I saw where a shark's tooth is replaced every eight days."

The arresting officer says, "Like clockwork or on average?"

The entertainer bum, his name is William, says, "What this means is that given the average shark life expectancy of twenty to twenty-five years—some of your dogfish sharks live to be a hundred, but let's bracket them as a statistical outlier—what this means is that sharks, an average shark, goes through thirty thousand teeth in a lifetime."

The arresting officer punches William in the ribs and says, "You're drunk and full of shit."

William doubles over with his hands cuffed behind his back. He says, "I may be drunk," but it's hard to hear because he's gasping.

The Police Commissioner says, "I can virtually guarantee you a bomb-free event."

Spray-painted graffiti on the sidewalk says, "Pooh v. Jaws."

Mr. Norman, breathing heavily by now, disappears into the lobby of the Roman Coliseum. Curtis is sleeping like a baby.

William wheezes and says, "Thirty thousand and that is the *truth*."

86

Another Essay That Did Not Win

LONESOME BvS BLUES NO. 3

(by the Last Folksinger)

I know, drummers come and drummers go
I had just never seen one go that fast
I'm three lines into the first verse
And I think I hear a symbol crash
So I turn around and there's an empty kit
Where Stevie used to sit
Man, he's beating his retreat
Got a front row seat
At the Darwin Dome
Yeah my drummer got snared

Ethan on bass starts falling behind
You know the second verse is same as the first
He's got those cartoon pinwheels in his eyes
He's thinking of the winner's purse
Wants to know who would win
When the paw meets the fin
Stevie's sticks still in the air

When Ethan decides to meet him there in Vegas
Hear that steady beat of four allegro feet
Now I got no rhythm, just the blues

So when I sing that bears and sharks are for the birds
Man, it's not a chorus
It's just me
Yeah it's not a chorus
It's just me

Martin's a pro on the piano
And he keeps his fingers on the keys
But by that third verse he's thinking
Shit, why them and not me?
Brenda is our backup singer
She joined the band last year
And maybe I should have known
That the harmony would end right here
Martin and Brenda, they hit the road
Now she's singing jingles, he's typing code
For the Man

So when I sing that BvS is a boar
It's not a chorus
It's just me
No it's not a chorus
It's just me

Well, we stumbled to the bridge
Just me and brave Claudine
But halfway across she stopped and
Threw down her tambourine
She sprinted stage left and said
She hoped Martin could fix that bear's head
Once and for all

The fourth verse has a lonely sound
It howls like wind through a crack
The band has abandoned me and

I'm getting bad feedback
Yeah the band couldn't refrain
And I'm getting bad feedback

So when I sing that BvS is bull
Hey, it's not a chorus
It's just me
And when I yell you're all sheep
It's no chorus
It's just me
It's just me

Let me introduce the band
It's just me
It's just me
It's just me

87

Cold Compress

Mr. Norman sneaks into the hotel room on the twenty-first floor. On Television things are either turning out OK or else they are getting messed up so that they can later turn out OK. Let's face it, an hour of OK would be boring and an hour of messed up would be depressing.

Mr. Norman undresses Curtis and tucks him into bed. It's been a long time since Mr. Norman has done this and it makes him feel, well, good, and also bad, too.

Matthew turns over in his sleep and says, "What?"

Murray Jay Siskind says, "Look past the violence, Jack. There is a wonderful brimming spirit of innocence and fun."

Mr. Norman wonders whether he should elevate Curtis's feet. Or maybe his head. Something should get elevated.

What the hell is a cold compress?

Tourniquet, splint, triage.

Mr. Norman gingerly removes the robot bounty hunter Band-Aid from Curtis's gunshot wound—wow, what a day it's been—and, after cleaning the wound with a wet tissue, puts on a new Band-Aid. The wound is healing nicely. This makes him (Mr. Norman) feel better.

Mr. Norman climbs into bed. Mrs. Norman sleeps while in her headphones a lady Ph.D. chants spinal maxims.

Drunk motorists honk their horns in the streets far below.

Curtis is peaceful, the covers pulled up to his chin. You must keep the patient warm.

Bump on the noggin.

Mr. Norman sleeps and in his restless dreams, there it is, Tele-Town, each Television a pixel, a million pixels forming a beacon in the neon night.

88

Expert Testimony

Without ever leaving my Houston apartment, I was able to get in touch with biological experts throughout the world. I didn't want just any old Ph.D. out there. First, I wanted animal people, not plant people. Second, I wanted vertebrate people. Lastly, I wanted them to be smiling in their Web site photographs. (I should add that I was also seeking good geographical distribution in terms of forest experts v. sea experts.) When I found experts out there on the Internet who met all of these requirements, I sent them electronic mail messages, asking who would win in a fight between a bear and a shark, given a relatively level playing field, etc. When your sink is broken, don't you call a plumber?

So I interviewed some experts. At least I *think* they're experts. Remember Curtis's good point in Chapter 30 about credibility and ethos. I mean, how do I really know these people have their Ph.D.'s in the biological sciences? Perhaps they just have Ph.D.'s in rhetoric. Perhaps they've just finished their coursework. Perhaps they've never even taken any coursework. Perhaps they're plumbers who read a lot or, far worse, plumbers who don't read much at all. What is it that makes me believe (for I *do* believe) that these Internet people are legitimate experts? Furthermore: Do *you* believe these people are experts? Do you trust their word *and* mine? Or maybe you believe that I believe them, but you don't believe them, in which case you trust my word but not my powers of discernment. Or maybe you, like my brother-in-law (a developer of the modern-day koan, *really*), think that I phrased the question poorly (see Chapter 10) and thus elicited slanted responses. Or maybe you believe that there are indeed Internet experts of all kinds out there, but that I did not really find and contact them, in which case you don't trust my word. You believe that I made up the experts and their commentary (below), just as you believe that I've made up so many of the things in this book, like the Vibra-Dream Plus and the Sovereign Nation of Las Vegas. Thorny issues, indeed, Curtis.

What can I say? I'm not a plumber, have not even taken any courses. I really did send electronic mail messages to people I thought were experts. It's true. Turns out not that many of them wrote me back. Maybe they didn't think the question was serious, which of course it was, which of course it wasn't. It was both real and fake, authentic and ironic.

But much to my delight and gratitude, a few of these smiling biologists did write me back (via electronic mail), and here's how they responded.

- A zoologist at the University of Florida says, "Hi. Why are you asking me? There is no clear-cut answer to this question. It would depend on the species of shark, the species of bear, and numerous other factors."

- A professor in the Evolution and Ecology Department at the University of California–Davis says, "I'd have to go with the shark, because if the water is deep enough for the shark to be able to breathe (let alone swim) the bear would probably be in too deep to be able to defend itself. Note that although some bears do a fair bit of swimming (e.g., polar bears), when swimming their paws and jaws are not in a position that would allow them to be used as offensive or defensive weapons when they are engaged in this activity."

- A biologist at Weber State University in Ogden, Utah, says, "Chris—I feel honored that I've been solicited, albeit at random! I guess the answer really depends on the species of bear and shark (I will assume you mean the biggest meanest shark). I have to think that even a polar bear wouldn't stand much of a chance against a big shark. The shark (such as a great white) would have the advantage of speed and size, not to mention bite radius. Now don't get me wrong, polar bears are no slouches either. But given your 'level playing field' I would have to put my money on a shark. But remember, it depends on the species!"

- A scientist at the Bell Museum of Natural History on the campus of the University of Minnesota says, "This sounds like some novel! In fact most sharks are marine animals whereas most bears are terrestrial animals. Thus, such an encounter is most unlikely, but assuming a large shark species (there are many species that would be small enough for the bear to bat them around with little risk) was involved in this fight, I think the salt of the marine environment would get in the bear's eyes, the bear would be out of its element in the water, and thus it would be no real match for the shark."

- A Ph.D. at a bear-related Web site says, "Chris, fun to think about. If a big bear could get its feet on the bottom and turn and bite, I would think it could do some damage and escape after being bitten. All hypothetical, of course. P.S.: I did hear of a black bear that swam 6 miles out into the Gulf of Mexico from Florida and then swam back. The boat followed the bear halfway back before leaving."

So on paper, at least, it looks like no contest. Three out of five (60 percent) experts say a shark would win easily. (Sixty percent is a landslide in presidential elections.) But listen, as the cliché goes, great sporting events are not played on paper, they're played on real fake grass in domed stadiums.

On *paper,* did North Carolina State have a chance against mighty Houston?

On *paper,* did the U.S. Olympic hockey team have a chance against the Russians or whomever they beat for the gold that one time when I was a kid?

On *paper,* did Joe Namath's Jets stand a chance in that Super Bowl?

On *paper,* did Taft have a prayer against Van Buren?

You just never know, head-lugged Cinderella could crash this party, her paws crammed into slippers, her pearly teeth dripping with gore.

89

Inside

Inside America is Las Vegas and inside Las Vegas is the Roman Coliseum Hotel and inside the Roman Coliseum Hotel is room MMCXXII and inside room MMCXXII is a double bed and inside the double bed is a man and a woman.

Wait: Who threw a blanket over the Televisions?

It's so dark.

Quiet, too, with the Complimentary Gladiator Earplugs. Just the faintest hum of violence and fun, out there. The faintest pulse. And vague shadow puppets loving or killing on the curtains, it's hard to tell.

So quiet and dark under the covers when the man rolls inside the woman, both of them not quite awake, that part of the night when this can happen.

She says, "Like that."

She whispers it. He can't hear her.

He says, "Sometimes I catch a glimpse."

She says, "I'm still alive."

Their wet faces are smashed together, eyes open in the total dark. They are speaking, unheard, simultaneously, through clenched teeth.

He says, "Like that?"

She says, "This could have been my story."

Which is true.

He says, "I don't even make the fake stuff. I just design it."

She says, "I saw you. Each time I was pregnant."

He says, "Do you know what I mean?"

She says, "I saw how you'd wait for me to sleep, then you'd crawl under the covers with that tiny flashlight and look at my belly. For hours."

He says, "Move this way a little."

She says, "I only pretended to be asleep. I knew what you were doing. For hours looking at my round belly, barely touching it with your fingers and lips."

It's all like a dream but it's not. The Vibra-Dream Plus and the UnPillow are nowhere to be seen.

She says, "The radio talk show host told me it was creepy and I should ask for a divorce."

He says, "Divorce?"

She says, "But it was sweet and I loved you for it."

There are seven cervical vertebrae, twelve thoracic vertebrae, five lumbar vertebrae, five sacral vertebrae, and four caudal or coccygeal vertebrae.

The man and the woman roll like experts.

He says, "Curtis is going to be OK."

She says, "It's not too late."

The man bites the woman's ear, sucks out the complimentary earplug.

He says, "Like that?"

She says, "Yes. Larry, yes."

90

Wait-and-See Attitude

Nine hours until Bear v. Shark II.

Can you feel the tension? Would you say there is an electricity in the air? Would you say it's crackling?

In the morning the patient opens his eyes, which is a good sign. He goes to the bathroom. He is up and moving around, this is good. He is not talking. He has made some noises, but not really any words. He dribbles juice substitute on himself. His balance is a little off. He has a big knot on the back of his skull.

An egg on the old noggin.

Corneybacteria causes a swollen head.

Mrs. Norman says, "Curtis, are you OK?"

Mr. Norman says, "Curt fell out of bed last night. I got up and put him back."

This is a lie, but.

Matthew says, "Oh, I remember him coming back to bed."

It's strange how a lie can so easily and quickly find verification.

Mr. Norman says, "He'll be OK."

Mrs. Norman says, "Maybe we should take him to a doctor."

Real fake chariots race around the hotel lobby, where the Normans enjoy their Continental Breakfast. Stoic members of the housekeeping staff exit the elevator, their togas swooshing.

Mr. Norman is scared of doctors, isn't everyone? Those machines.

You turn them on and they say something—cancer or a stroke—and then you have cancer or a stroke and you start to feel terrible. The machines speak and the doctors just translate and there is no arguing. It's the final word and you might die. Mr. Norman is adopting a wait-and-see attitude on this one.

Matthew says, "Curt, can I have your cream-filled donut if you're not going to eat it?"

Curtis says, well, nothing.

91

Train of Thought

Know that paper I wrote on Bear v. Shark?
The one you got off the Internet?
Yeah.
The one about how the bear is the ego and the shark is the id?
Yeah.
Froyd.
I got a D.
Jesus, that was the best paper out of all of them.
Teacher said he couldn't follow my *train of thought.*
What's a train of thought?
My train of thought, that's what he said.
A train. *Of thought.*
Yeah, he couldn't follow it.
And he wanted to?
Follow it?
Yeah.
I guess so.
He wanted to follow your so-called *train of thought,* but he couldn't.
Hold on, I got another call.

A train of thought, it would seem, is a positive thing. One wants to have a train of thought so that others can follow it. A train made entirely of thought. A thought train, with teachers in tow.

I'm back. You there?

What is *porridge,* anyway?

What's a train got to do with it?

A train is an outmoded form of transportation.

That's what I'm saying.

It's slow and smoky.

Heavy, loud.

Well if slow and smoky thoughts are good, then I'm a damn idiot severe.

It's true.

Damn boy genius, if smoky thinking's the yardstick.

What we're talking about here is number one, why would I want a train of thought, number two, why would he want to follow it, and number three.

Number three is why would you want a damn train of thought in the first place when there's all kinds of thought vehicles out there that are faster and more efficient and constructed especially for the modern reader.

Today's hectic world.

Who the hell wants to sit still at a thought crossing and just watch those linked ideas roll by?

Hold on, I got another call.

92

The Museum of Las Vegas Secession

It's on to the Museum of Las Vegas Secession, remember, that huge and impressively amusing educational complex. But it's hard for the Normans to get very excited about the museum, what with the Event looming in the near future.

It seems that the thousands of other people at the museum feel the same way. People are nervous, on edge. Everyone is just wandering around, killing time, waiting.

Who would win in a fight between a bear and a shark?

I mean, think about it, if a bear (with a normal-sized head) and a shark had a conflict that they could not settle peaceably . . . who would win?

I'd eat broken glass for a ticket, I would.

The Virtual Water Park is fun because you don't get wet for real.

The Original Gambling Monkey is pretty amazing. He plays blackjack and poker, mostly. But here's what they never tell you in the ads: The monkey is a *terrible* gambler. He almost always loses, it's like he doesn't even understand the rules or the purpose.

The World's Largest Billboard is immense, to be sure, but a bit of a letdown. It's not as big as it looks on the Internet. Pictures can lie.

Mr. Norman holds Curtis's hand as the family walks around the museum, which is a nice thing that he hasn't done in a long time.

Curtis walks slowly and a bit unsteadily, staring straight ahead. He seems to be getting much better. He eats cotton candy and rubs some of it in his hair. Not once at the museum does he run off or get lost or get shot.

There is a petting zoo with a toothless, sedated bear with glassy eyes and tangled fur. It lies on its side taking shallow breaths while the children poke it. There is also a shark, apparently, but it won't come out from behind a plastic rock.

Mr. Norman leans down to Curtis and says, "You ready for tonight, little man?"

Docents in animal masks make children run and cry.

He (Mr. Norman) says, "You think the shark will get what's coming to him?"

Curtis doesn't say anything.

Matthew says, "No way, Dad."

A sign says, "The brave men and women who settled this country came here seeking a better way of life."

A sign says, "Coming tomorrow: Bear v. Shark II: A Historical Perspective."

A man on a pay phone says, "You fucking *promised* me you'd have the detonator."

Matthew says, "Sucks you have to wait for history."

93

Oral Vacuum

There is a shark out there in the ocean called a cookie-cutter shark. *Isistius brasiliensis.* Even though it is pretty clearly an Internet hoax, I'm going to assume that it's real, as I assume American astronauts landed on the moon, as I assume Greenland exists, as I assume the biological experts in Chapter 88 really have their Ph.D.'s. Call me gullible. I've seen Internet pictures of the cookie-cutter shark. This is not a pretty animal—creepy eyes and a godawful mouth—but still, it doesn't look like some terror of the deep. Not the great white, the so-called man-eater, not 50 feet long like the whale shark. It's cigar-shaped, eel-like, about 50 cm in length, max. (As any decent dashboard will tell you, that's about 20 inches long.) And cookie-cutter shark is such a harmless name, a fun name, even, who doesn't like cookies?, my friends and I love them, except here's the thing: do you know why it's called that? What this shark does is attach itself to some much larger creature, sometimes another shark, with its thick, "suctorial" lips and long, sharp teeth, and then it spins hard in order to rip out a cookie-shaped plug of flesh from the larger animal. This plug is sometimes referred to as a "flesh cookie." Cookie-cutter sharks have very strong basihyals (see above) and mighty rectus cervicis throat muscles in order to create a powerful "oral vacuum." A recent theory suggests that the cookie-cutter shark's markings trick other, larger fish into thinking it is a very small fish. When the larger fish attacks this "very small fish," the cookie-cutter turns and lunges at the lunger, using the larger fish's forward motion to help rip out the plug of flesh, the cookie. I might add that at one site there is talk of cookie-cutter sharks cratering the sturdy sonar domes of nuclear submarines.

So say you're a big fish. This seemingly harmless creature with the fun name lies to you, assaults you with a powerful oral vacuum, and then makes a hole in you forever.

Damn right it's a metaphor.

94

Big Afternoon

Tell about the Big Afternoon leading up to the Big Event.

Five hours, four hours, three hours, two hours . . .

Slow down. Use some striking images, some poignant details. What's the weather like?

Sunny. Hot. Hot as . . . I don't know.

What else?

What's to say? I'd skip it if you'd let me.

I won't let you.

I know.

Tell it.

I don't know, a nap. Yes, a family nap. Boy, they sure are tired, those Normans.

C'mon.

It's true. It's really true, now that I think about it.

Boring.

So.

Boring is bad.

Not all of life can be so entertaining.

What about art? What about novels?

Depends.

Tell about Curtis.

He's asleep like the others.

Something's wrong with him. There's a problem here. There's a crisis, a conflict.

We're adopting a wait-and-see attitude.

What's going to happen to him?

I, like sharks and most other fishes, cannot see the future.

They're all asleep.

Yes. Well. Mr. Norman isn't asleep. He can't sleep. He keeps looking over to see if Curtis is still breathing.

And is he?

Breathing?

Yes.

Yes.

Boring. But outside, on the streets of Las Vegas, it's like a big party or something, right? People tailgating and drinking and celebrating and getting ready. A festive, jubilant atmosphere. Some fights breaking out between bear and shark factions. Right?

But see, that's the thing, it's not a party. Nobody is out on the street, almost nobody. It's hot and bright and empty out there. Kind of creepy. People are lying low, staying quiet. It's never like this in Las Vegas, but today it is. It just doesn't look right. You need people to make this place look right. Without people, it looks.

Deserted?

Worse than deserted. Egregious. At BvS: The Theme Park there are no lines. It's never been easier to ride those upside-down rides. There are three people on The Mama's Den and maybe three more on The Unlevel Playing Field. They're all screaming with their hands in the air like you're supposed to, but you can tell their hearts aren't in it. One might say that a *pall* has *descended*.

Hey you've got your religion and I've got mine.

Of course.

Family nap and empty streets.

That's what I'm saying, yes.

No wonder nobody reads anymore. So what should I do the rest of the day?

I don't know, flip through a celebrity magazine or watch a sporting event.

I can't. I'm too antsy and restless about tonight.

Oh well.

Hey, would you care for a flesh cookie?

No thanks.

Didn't someone die one time on The Mama's Den?

You're thinking of Goldilocks's Nightmare. The guy was too tall and his head just.

Say, who would win in a fight between a bear and a shark?

Stay tuned, I reckon.

95

The War of Nature

A free, crowded, and eerily quiet shuttle ride down to the Darwin Dome.

These are common folk on the shuttle, the lottery winners. Their T-shirts are loud and brash, but their faces are blank, even grim.

Grim, with one hour remaining before Bear v. Shark II: The War of Nature. What gives?

Mr. Norman wonders if *his* face is grim. And if his face is grim, does that mean he's *feeling* grim, too? He intentionally makes a grim face, and then thinks about how much work it took. If it was relatively easy to make a grim face from his regular, ground-state face, then maybe his face was already pretty far on toward grim, and thus maybe he is feeling grim. If his face had to go a long way to make a grim face, then maybe he is the opposite of grim, happy or something.

Step One: Make a grim face.

Step Two: Measure the difference between regular face and grim face.

Step Three: Determine your emotional state.

Mrs. Norman says, "Honey, what are you doing?"

This isn't easy, and it really isn't as scientific as it seems. There's room for human error here. Subjectivity creeps back in.

Curtis sits in his father's lap. Under each of his eyes is a shiny blue crescent of bruise. Blue and shiny, like an insect's wings. Back at the hotel Matthew swore he heard Curtis say something, some words, not English words, really, but an utterance of some type. The child is coming around.

If you are faced with a bear in a threatening situation, remain calm and still. Sometimes playing dead works. The *last* thing you want to do is run away. Bears are fast.

A T-shirt says, "Real men have coarse, thick fur."

Another T-shirt says, "Hibernation is for pussies."

Grim faces.

Darwin, the nineteenth-century scientist, says, in the penultimate sentence of his *On the Origin of Species,* "Thus, from the war of nature, from famine and death, the most exalted object which we are capable of conceiving, namely, the production of the higher animals, directly follows."

Civic Leaders and Captains of Industry say, "I don't much care for Darwin on origins, but I like what he has to say about competition."

And there it is, folks, the Darwin Dome, brilliant in the August sun. A cathedral and a crucible.

The shuttle driver, an anarchist with some vague cult ties, says, "Well, here we are."

Mrs. Norman says, "Isn't it something?"

From his father's lap, Curtis stares out the bullet-proof shuttle windows at the desert arena.

The dictionary says dome means house of God.

96

Bear v. Shark: The Index

abortion, 60
Adams, Grizzly, 21
Agassi, Andre, 242
American ear, broad, flapping, 112
American Vacation, 161, 166, 167–68, 171, 174
announcement, public service, 66
Antichafe Flap, patented, 123
Aristotle, 164
Ark, Noah's, 137
Asians, 127
Astroturf, 184, 207
Atlanta 24, Carolina 14
atmosphere:
    festive and jubilant, 189, 231
    foreboding, 170
    grim, 233–34
author's apartment, 116

Babble Blocker, 23–24
baby, lost, 79, 81, 82, 83
back to you, Brock, 152
Backacher, Chris, 171

Badchildren, Chris, 173
Bandleader, Chris, 166
Barthelme, Donald, 116
Barthes, Roland, 120
bears:
    Bear Killer, 73, 74, 113
    cabaret, 144
    churlish, 130
    fur, 79, 107, 141, 227, 248
    head, large, 248–49
    head-lugged, 130, 219
    head, small, 78
    hibernation, 83, 134, 135, 186, 234
    invisible, 72
    meat, 242
    milk, 245
    paws, 125, 218, 219
    pipin' swords, 113
    porn, 116, 117
    running downhill, 168
    sark, 62
    slippers, 219

bears (*cont.*)
  speed, 219
  swimming, 218
  syrup, love of, 125
  teeth, 94, 219, 249
  verbs, 131
Bear v. Shark:
  I, 53, 78, 93–94, 157, 166, 191,
    205, 249
  II, 17, 43, 70, 75, 105, 127, 129,
    150, 181, 188, 191, 201, 210,
    222, 227, 233
  III, 246–47
  action figures, 99, 146
  Blues No. 3, 212
  Breakfast Cereal, The, 42–43
  Classic Game of Strategy and
    Entertainment, The, 99
  cone, the, 196
  essay, the, 77
  How to Talk to Your Children about
    Bear v. Shark, 146
  index, the, 235
  insider's story, the, 93–94
  license plates, personalized, 100
  logo, the, 26, 191
  novel, the, 155
  On Ice, 57
  origins, 53–54
  parties, 251
  preface, the, 11
  question, the, 32
  quiz, the, 134–35
  rising action, the, 151–53
  Tale of the Tape, The, 28
  Talk Radio, 60, 61–63
  Theme Park, The, 231
  T-shirt, 78
bees, killer, 77
birds, fake, 19, 26, 33
bivouac, scenic, 48–49, 176

Blackletter, Chris, 161
boards:
  bill, 44, 67, 81, 82, 86, 104, 148
    (*see also* Jesus)
  dash, 56, 95, 96, 106, 173, 228
bombs, 184, 205–6, 211, 250
boot, cowboy, 169
boy:
  crippled, 184–85
  drowning, 133
breakfast:
  analytic, 133
  Continental, 133, 222
  on a stick, 173
brother-in-law, my, 165, 218
Buffalo 17, Baltimore 14
butt, perfect, 11
'Bye, Dale, 63

cake, chocolate, 20–21, 23–24
Calvino, Italo, 116
carrots, wavy, 162
chinchilla, 119
chlorine, 122
Cleveland 17, New Orleans 10
cockfights, 66, 98
Comedy, Situation, 66, 192
context, pseudo, 92
cookies:
  flesh, 228
  ginger, 148
costumes, furry, 141
cricket, dead, 122
cults, 192–93, 199, 205–7, 234
Curtis's knees, 152–53, 156

Darwin, Charles, 33, 43, 54, 234, 242
Darwin Dome, 44, 70–71, 145, 153,
    181, 182, 193, 197, 199, 206,
    207, 212, 233, 234, 241–42,
    249, 250

Debate, Ten-Second, 59–60
delay, seven-second, 136
democracy, 60, 165
Denver 34, Minnesota 31
depression, 171, 205
desire, refracted, 122
despot, beneficent (*see* boards, dash)
dew point (*see* weather)
disaster, passenger train, 55
disciples, the, 137, 138
disease:
    cancer, 121, 144–45, 223
    Dutch Elm, 64
    freshwater, 192–93
    gum, 75
dog:
    Last Folksinger's, 47
    wiener, 124
Dorfman, Ariel, 108
Dutch, the, 38, 64–65, 77, 88, 97

earplugs, complimentary, 220
Edison, Thomas, 82–83
electronic equipment, fake,
    25–26
entertainers, homeless, 201, 210
entertainment exhaust, 148–50
experts, 23, 54, 217–19, 221, 228
eyes:
    funny, 74
    weird, 108, 183

face, grim, 233–34
feelings, palpable, 100–102
fisherman, well-read, 75
Florentine, banana, 65
Folksinger, Last, 47, 57, 212
Food Marts, 106, 148
footage:
    interesting, 37
    stock, 38, 124

fork fork fork, 111
French and Indian War, 115
Freud, Sigmund, 131
Frost, Robert, 106
Frozen Dinner Rolls, Insta-Bake
    (*see* Curtis's knees)

Gambling Monkey, World's Original,
    45, 226
gardener (*see* Dutch, the)
gas, inert, 198, 201, 211
gaskin, 109, 110
ghost, 161, 173
gills, bleeding, 194, 201
Goldilocks's Nightmare, 232
grace, shredded, 104
Green Bay 27, Seattle 20
Green Paint, 121, 176
guarantee, four-minute, 28
Guard, National, 171
guy:
    from other booth, 81–83
    from Pump 22, 107–8

hair, unwanted, 20
hand:
    invisible, 171
    of the diligent, 241–42
HardCorp, 54, 70, 78, 93, 97, 172,
    173, 242, 248
Hart, Owen, 155
hash, canned, 152
Hernia Soda, 59, 127–28, 178
hoax (*see* Internet)
hoboes, 56, 81
hockey team, U.S. Olympic, 219
hogshead, 96
Hollis, Rev., 137–39
Holmes:
    Oliver Wendell, 84
    Sherlock, 84

hookers, 201
hoosegow (*see* prison)
horse, pommel, 109
human spirit, triumph of, 210
Huxley, Aldous, 54, 101

ich, 188, 194, 195
Indianapolis 14, Dallas 13
Internet, 17, 24, 34, 39, 48, 72–75,
      78, 81, 99, 111, 113, 115, 118,
      119, 144, 146, 165–67, 176,
      188, 199, 210, 217–18, 224,
      226, 228, 249
irony, 12, 116, 149

Jacksonville 40, Cincinnati 17
Jesus:
    on a billboard, 82
    on the Darwin Dome, 242
join join join, 111
jokes, 72, 116
judge, TV commercial, 20
jump, Curtis, 207

Kansas City 13, San Diego 9
King, Martin Luther, 242
knitting, electronic, 67–68
knock, knock, 72
knot:
    Accordion, 113, 250
    Gordian, 94
    Gordon, 113
    granny, 114
    Guardian, 113, 174
koan, 54, 218

Las Vegas, 33, 38, 44, 45, 47, 54, 59,
      69, 70, 97, 157, 169, 183, 184,
      190, 199–200, 226–27
lawn, chipped and faded, 251
lawyer, lady, 20–21, 23

license plates, personalized, 100
Lindbergh, Charles, 18, 85, 189
Link, Breakfast, 104
linoleum, 12
Lloyd, 45–46
Lloyd's mother, 45–46, 251
Look past the violence, Jack, 215
love, flood of, 30

marble, lucky, 46
Meredith, Dr. Sara, 61–63
Miami 30, Chicago 13
microcoils, interlocked, 30
Mindy's ex-boyfriend Nate, 53
mockery, 116
Moody, Rick, 163
Moore, Lorrie, 163
moralism, 116
motorists, drunk, 210–11, 215
mouse:
    dead, 43, 51, 192
    foolhardy, 42
Munson, Rev. Marty, 40–41
Museum of Las Vegas Secession, The,
    45, 226–27

Namath, Joe, 219
nausea, 104, 114
neon, 197
Net Nook, 34, 38
New England 24, Arizona 23
New York Giants 9, Philadelphia 7
nine yards, the whole, 108
noggin, bump on the, 210, 216, 222

oriole bolus, 125
outing, father-son, 198

pains, fruitless, 104
Pants, Sexy, 140, 151
parlor, 15, 35

Personality, Television, 26, 40, 101, 120

Petty, Richard, 62

pillow:
cordless vibrating, 16–17, 51, 198
UnPillow, 31, 221

Planet Peanut Brittle, 67–68

plumbers, 217–18

police, 81, 90, 211, 241

polls, recent, 97–98, 101

porridge, 35, 225

Postman, Neil, 59, 92, 183, 249

posture, 31, 33, 51, 56, 58, 98, 108, 163, 192, 250

Princess Adelaide, 112

prison:
cabbage, 183
Las Vegas, 183, 199
sex, 50, 122

Pynchon, Thomas, 163, 167

racehorse, 109

Razor, Ockham's, 173

rhetoric, 161–65, 217

Richards, I. A., 164

Round-Eyed Sons of the Knightly Order, 133

sandwich, dick, 52

satire, 116

Saunders, George, 163

scrotum, underneath the, 156

sequitur, non, 120

sex (*see* prison)

Shakespeare, 129–31, 249

sharks:
belly, 124
bite radius, 219
cookie-cutter, 228–29
dogfish, 211
erogenous zone, 86
fins, 53, 61–63, 77, 86, 195
hat, 57
maw and gulf, 130
neck, 133
pajamas, 34
ravined, 130, 191
skin, 86
sleep, 81–83
swimming backward, 166
teeth, 29, 53, 62, 72, 75, 86, 94, 211, 228, 249
tongue, 28, 134, 203, 208–9

shower cap, 197, 202

Shut up, Helen, 60

silence, moment of, 248

Siskind, Murray Jay, 215

snacks:
cheese, 104
meat, 70, 71, 97

Spartacus, 167

Sport Utility Vehicle, 38, 44, 50, 51, 52, 56, 89, 90, 95, 106, 107, 108, 164, 168, 171, 173, 175, 176, 184

squirrel eater, 165

Sterno, 172

St. Louis 28, Tennessee 20

Taft, William Howard, 93–94, 101–2, 219

Tampa Bay 20, Detroit 17

TeleTown, 48–49, 145, 148–50, 151, 152, 173, 174–76, 189, 216, 250

Television:
commercials, 20, 109, 157, 172, 210, 244
ESP TV, 58, 108
old, 22, 35, 58, 156
Outrageous Accomplishments Network, 25

Television (*cont.*)
    PayView, 97, 185, 248, 251
    Prison Network, 50
    Pundit Network, 27
    on staircase, 34, 37, 38
    see also weather
Television Room:
    small, 24, 64
    large, 17
Thigpen, Elton, 54
Thoreau, Henry David, 73, 74,
    166
toga, 167, 188, 222
tongue, swollen, 68–69
topiary, artichoke, 162
truth, bloody meat of, 87

unrest, civil, 166

Van Buren, Martin, 93–94, 101–2,
    112, 219
vertebrae (*see* posture)
village:
    French, 75
    global, 60
Virtual Water Park, World's
    Funnest, 44, 226
visit, conjugal, 50

Wallace, David Foster, 43, 149, 163
Wall of China, Great, 33
War of the Worlds, The, 154
Washington 34, Los Angeles 24
waterfall, 157
weapons:
    battle-ax, 44
    gun, derringer, 44
    gun, lightning, 81
    gun, turquoise, 151–52
    halberd, 74
    harpoon, 44
    ice pick, 45
    machete, 43
    pocket knife, contraband, 183
    scythe, 43
    see also bombs
weather:
    Bear Index, 38
    clouds, cumulative, 44
    dew point, 37–38
    Extreme Weather, 34, 37, 57
    fish-clouds, bloated, 44
    hot as . . . I don't know, 230
    sun, chemical, 119
    Tsunami Tsurvival!, 37
    Weather Europe, 33–34, 39
    Weather Network, 34
    Weather Network Plus, 34
Welles, Orson, 154
Wells, H. G., 154
Wittgenstein, 84–85
world:
    arid, 87–88
    dog-eat-dog, 181
    hectic, 28, 40, 42, 67, 107, 170,
        225, 245
    natural, 147, 249
    violent, 147
wrestling, professional, 155

yes, ma'am, 24, 137, 241, 250

Zen, Extreme, 26
zoo, petting, 227

97

The Hand of the Diligent

Forty-one minutes.

If a bear and a shark.

There are picketers and protesters outside the Dome. They have their chants and their signs. They've been watching too much American Television. Some people throw rocks at them. The unrestful inciting unrest.

One picketer's sign says, "Let a man meet a she-bear robbed of her cubs, rather than a fool in his folly (Proverbs 17.12)."

Another picketer's sign says, "Like a charging bear is a wicked ruler over a poor people (Proverbs 28.15)."

Another picketer's sign says, "Woe to you who desire the day of the LORD! It is darkness, and not light; as if a man fled from a lion, and a bear met him (Amos 5.19)."

The Bible is pretty quiet when it comes to sharks.

Las Vegas police members round up these zealots and scofflaws in a big truck and take them somewhere. What do you think this is—America?

Some punk in a chocolate cake costume climbs to the top of the Dome with a dog and a guitar. A crowd gathers outside the Dome to watch and listen and videotape. Nobody knows what the cake is singing about. Not once does he say *Yes, ma'am,* and people start to boo. Even the protesters in the police truck are booing the cake. The cake sings two and a half folksongs before LV's finest catch him, cuff him, and smash his guitar in the bright glinting light.

The crowd cheers, then disappears into the dark arena.

The Darwin Dome has four main entrances. On the north side, fans enter under an enormous arch made by statues of Charles Darwin and Jesus holding hands. On the east, fans enter under an enormous arch made by statues of Charles Darwin and Andre Agassi holding hands. On the south side, fans enter under an enormous arch made by statues of Charles Darwin and Martin Luther King Jr. holding hands. On the west, fans enter under an enormous arch made by statues of Charles Darwin and HardCorp CEO William T. "Ducky" Riggins III holding hands.

The Normans enter on the north side. Mrs. Norman holds Matthew's hand. Mr. Norman holds Curtis's hand. Darwin holds Jesus' hand.

A plaque underneath the Darwin statue says, "But as all groups cannot thus succeed in increasing in size, for the world would not hold them, the more dominant groups beat the less dominant."

A plaque underneath the Jesus statue says, "A slack hand causes poverty, but the hand of the diligent makes rich."

There's no reason these guys couldn't get along.

The Normans climb switchback ramps, they're high up with the Sea-n-Lea winners. Scholastic success can get you in the door, but it takes a little something more to get a ringside seat or a luxury box.

Mrs. Norman says, "Larry, if he's not feeling better by tomorrow, I think we better take him somewhere."

The Normans, well, Matthew and the parents, anyway, keep seeing people that look vaguely famous. You want to smile and wave at these people because you think you know them, you *do* know them, in fact, and you love them, they are a big part of your life, but here's the thing: They don't know you!

Things are for sale, plenty of things. Beer and shark meat and bear meat and popcorn and T-shirts and baseball caps and key chains and Styrofoam No. 1 hands and mixed drinks and commemorative pins and belt buckles and stuffed animals and other souvenirs, memorabilia, knickknacks, bricabrac, trinkets, gewgaws, cheap plastic shit made in Taiwan.

Where is Taiwan, exactly?

You just know there's something called the Beer-n-Bear Special and something else called the Great White Wiener and something else called Bearbecue.

And of course there are Gambling Stations. The bear is a slight favorite. The revenge factor.

People are speaking in hushed voices. The whole thing has a feel that is different from the feel that they expected the whole thing to have.

Mrs. Norman says, "What?"

Matthew clings tight to his mother's hand. He says, "This place is so big."

Mr. Norman says, "You doing OK, Curt?"

Curtis stays pretty quiet.

A sportscaster says, "I had a chance to take a peek at the bear and the shark earlier today, Rich, and let me tell you, I wouldn't want to run across either of them in a dark alley."

The clock says 23 minutes.

Mrs. Norman says, "We better find our seats."

It's a sad cake and a dog in that police truck.

98

Bear Milk

A commercial.

Pays the bills, builds suspense.

Telephone rings, Cute Young Mother, tastefully breast-feeding her infant in a warmly lit and tasteful Television room, answers.

She (Cute Young Mother) says, "Hello?"

Older Sister, also cute, more rugged, tomboyish, roughing it in some exotic locale, unmarried, worldly, not ready to settle down, don't fence her in. We are to understand from foliage and bird noises and no-nonsense ponytail and khaki vest with numerous pockets that she is working in a foreign country, some sort of nature job, would love to be home to see her sister and new baby but can't, she's got career responsibilities. You think monkeys, but there are none in sight. The phone line is clear, this could be a phone company commercial, bringing people together, but it is not.

She (Older Sister) says, "How's my kid sister?"

CYM says, "Oh, Molly, I wish you could be here."

Molly says, "Me, too, Sis. I'll be there soon. How's my brand-new niece?"

Sis says, "She's beautiful and wonderful. I just sat down to feed her when you called."

There is a small pause here.

Molly, concerned, says, "Sis, you're not breast-feeding, are you?"

Sis, just a trace of worry in her voice, says, "Yes, Molly, I am. Why?"

Molly says, "I just thought you would be using bear milk, that's all."

Sis, chuckling but still a bit nervous—this is a baby we're talking about here, completely helpless, everyone wants to do the right thing for the baby, it needs you to make sound developmental decisions—Sis says, "But Molly, human babies have always been raised with human milk."

Molly, amidst exotic animal noises, says, "Sis, in today's hectic, competitive world, human milk just doesn't cut it. Human milk is fine for average children, but truly exceptional children like my niece need more. . . ."

Cut now to a laboratory with busy white-coated actors bustling in the background. There are test tubes that clearly show. There is a bar graph that clearly shows. There is a Daytime Drama Star in a white coat who clearly shows. Turns out bear milk is 46 percent fat, while human milk is a paltry 4 percent fat. Turns out that bear cubs, relatively speaking, are the smallest of mammals when born, only 1/420th the weight of their mother. Human babies, in comparison, are 1/20th the weight of their mother. So how do bear cubs grow up so fast to be so strong and fast and mean? That's right, bear milk. Damn rocket fuel, that stuff.

Cut back to Cute Young Mother feeding a warm bottle of bear milk to her happy and remarkably healthy infant.

The doorbell rings and it's Molly! Home from the jungle to see her niece for the first time, her niece who is destined to be strong and extraordinary, don't we all want what's best for our children, do we dare settle for less?

The embrace.

"Oh, what an angel! And so big and exceptional-looking!"

"Big sister always knew best."

Laughter.

What I'm getting at is everything turns out OK.

99

Bear v. Shark III:
The Third Coming

Shit, for that kind of money, if Miami wants us, Miami's got us.

Miami wants us, sir.

We'll need a dome.

They say it's no problem.

Done deal, then.

I'll let them know, sir. We'll schedule a meeting to hammer out the details.

Maybe we can shake it up this time. You know, call it Shark v. Bear or something.

I think that would be a mistake, sir.

SvB3: The Third Time's the Harm! What do you think?

We can discuss the finer points later, sir.

Or I don't know, make them three times as big, or make it three-on-three or something.

Sir, change is sometimes dangerous. Our marketing research shows that people love their BvS just the way it is.

Yeah, I guess so.

We've got an excellent product, sir.

And not a bad profit, either.

Quite true, sir.

Hey wait, what if we used a real bear and a real shark, and passed them off as fake? We could save a shitload of money.

We've thought about that, sir. But there is concern that a real bear and a real shark would not be real enough to be convincingly fake.

Real would be too fake?

Real would be too real, sir, which would be fake, but not in a real way.

Real is not real enough.

Exactly, sir.

You're probably right.

But I think we do need to change the time frame, sir.

Explain.

Two years is simply too long to wait. People start shooting themselves in the heads and beating up their kids. We've got to come back sooner.

OK, we can do eighteen months.

Sir, I'm thinking more like eight months, an April bout.

That's soon.

Our research shows that eight months is optimal. We can do tie-ins to Easter, the whole resurrection theme.

That's real soon.

Yes, sir, but I think we can swing it.

A spring fight, though, I like it.

Yes, sir.

Here's the thing.

Yes, sir.

If there's a third fight.

Yes, sir.

And the shark won the first fight.

Yes, sir.

Then.

Sir, I don't think the programmers are going to like that.

Well, do you think the programmers like having jobs?

I'll talk to them, sir.

100

And Now This

The Normans in their seats, high above the ring.

Sixty-five thousand fans and tens of millions more worldwide on PayView.

Oh man, not too long now until a bear and a shark get in a fight and who would win if they did.

The announcer says, "HardCorp asks that you take a moment of silence to pray for American troops."

The Vice President of Las Vegas says, "Nobody told us about no moment of silence."

The moment is, well, silent. Or close. Not very.

One thinks of wind-kissed meadows. One thinks of bomb shelters.

And then the lights go out and the loud extreme music comes on.

The announcer says, "Welcome, fight fans, to the Greatest Spectacle in Recorded History."

Then a dancing spotlight on the ring. Some crisscrossing lasers. There is clear, blue water, some small trees and brush, a sandy shore.

A person would not be alarmed to see either a bear or a shark in this setting. This is a level playing field.

The announcer says, "In one corner, the challenger, a large mammal of the family Ursidae, found almost exclusively in the Northern Hemisphere, with a large head, a bulky body, short and powerful and clawed limbs, and coarse, thick fur, standing almost nine feet tall and weighing more than 1,500 pounds, Shakespeare's darling, well rested and looking for revenge . . . the *BEAR*!"

Stunned and terrified fans clap as a gigantic bear materializes in one corner of the ring. Angry drool, realer than life, drops in strings from its truth-white teeth.

The bear's head is, well, enormous. One Internet site will call it "slightly enlarged." Another will call it "grotesque in its dimensions." Another will call it "roughly proportionate to the body." Another will call it "understandably and justly bloated given the debacle of Bear v. Shark I." And so on.

Decide for yourself.

Mr. Norman is feeling a little queasy. He sets down his Bearrito.

The sports announcer says, "Wow, what a specimen, Rich."

The ringside announcer says, "In the other corner, twelve feet long with six senses, multiple rows of triangular, razor-sharp teeth, a tough, cartilaginous exterior, if it stops swimming it sinks, a legendary predator, unmentioned in the Bible, absent from the night sky, ravined as all get-out, the undisputed champion of BvS . . . the *SHARK*!"

Some clapping, some booing, as the shark materializes, menacingly, in the opposite corner. Matthew is pale in the dark. He doesn't clap.

Some people, a few people, leave their seats and head down the aisles. Of these, some are seeking a rest room, but others are leaving the Dome, they can't say exactly why, but they have to get out of there. Years later a social scientist will seek these people out for interviews, but he will find no trace of them.

And then.

And then there's a bell and the bear and shark *engage*.

Bear and shark, natural and sworn enemies, set upon each other with a ferocious and violent and long-standing enmity. The natural world is horrific, there's no denying it.

And then the screaming.

Flesh is shredded, bones shatter.

The bear roars and shrieks. The shark makes some awful noise like nobody has ever heard before.

Neil Postman says, "Who is prepared to take arms against a sea of amusements?"

Mr. Norman looks to his left, where Matthew and Mrs. Norman are seated.

Shark-loving Matthew, like so many others in the Dome, has his face buried in his hands. He is wailing and biting his palms.

A small and badly placed bomb goes off in Section 234, far away from the Event. Amateur work, but the blast looks awesome.

Mrs. Norman appears to be passed out against the back of her seat. She is remiss in her posture. Her gum with long-lasting flavor has fallen out of her mouth and is stuck to the commemorative pin on her blouse. Her eyes are rolled back in her head. She quivers, in shock.

Down in the ring it is realer than life.

The blood geysers and spouts. Cartilage in ribbons.

Red-gilled fish gasp for air in the lobby of the Roman Coliseum.

Mr. Norman looks to his right, where his youngest son is sitting. Curtis stares at the Event with bruised, watery eyes, a blank, drooling face. There are still pink wisps of cotton candy in his tousled hair. A sticky Finsicle melts in his pudgy hands.

Accordion knot.

His T-shirt says, "I won the Bear v. Shark essay contest and you didn't."

Mr. Norman says, "Curtis?"

He says, "Buddy?"

The sports announcer says, "I think we all expected a good fight, but none of us, Rich, none of us expected . . . *this.*"

Bloody and innocent and nonfamous bomb victims in Section 234 say, "Help." They try to say it.

Curtis makes a noise with his mouth. Did he just say, *"Yes, ma'am"*? Mr. Norman thinks the child said, "Yes, ma'am." Was it that or just some nonsense phrase?

The bear's arm, realer than life, is torn from its bulky body. The shark looks to have been caught in a helicopter blade. The animals writhe. There is glistening meat.

In TeleTown they wait. They're always looking for new members in the unique, self-sustaining community.

In the dark Mr. Norman thinks he sees the corners of Curtis's mouth turn up slightly. Is this kid smiling? Is he happy and well adjusted? Is Mr. Norman the World's Greatest Dad, as it says on three Father's Day coffee mugs back home in America? Who would win in a fight between Mr. Norman and other kids' dads?

Mr. Norman says, "Curtis, you in there, pal?"

He says, "Please, son."

In America, Bear v. Shark parties grow hushed and anxious. Guests thank hosts quietly and slip out. This isn't like the Super Bowl. In their homes millions of Americans stare at PayView in silence. This is what they paid for. This is what they were told to want and this is what they wanted.

In America, Lloyd's mother won't let him watch. The boy is outside alone, playing imaginary jacks on the faded lawn. Threesies, Foursies, Fivesies.

Curtis stares on, transfixed by the Spectacle. He is delighted by the advances in entertainment technology. He is blissful, serene, a happy kid from the Mainland.

Or else the child's brain is damaged, vegetable dead, it's hard to tell, Walt.

But usually these things turn out OK, they do.